George Moore

Vain Fortune

A Novel

George Moore

Vain Fortune
A Novel

ISBN/EAN: 9783337001872

Printed in Europe, USA, Canada, Australia, Japan

Cover: Foto ©Andreas Hilbeck / pixelio.de

More available books at **www.hansebooks.com**

"SHE SLIPPED ON HER KNEES, AND BURST INTO A PASSIONATE FIT OF WEEPING."

VAIN FORTUNE

·A NOVEL BY ⸪

GEORGE MOORE

WITH FIVE ILLUSTRATIONS BY
MAURICE GREIFFENHAGEN

NEW EDITION
COMPLETELY
REVISED

LONDON: WALTER SCOTT, LTD.

PATERNOSTER SQUARE

1895

Edinburgh : T. and A. CONSTABLE, Printers to Her Majesty

PREFATORY NOTE

I HOPE it will not seem presumptuous to ask my critics to treat this new edition of *Vain Fortune* as a new book : for it is a new book. The first edition was kindly noticed, but it attracted little attention, and very rightly, for the story as told therein was thin and insipid ; and when Messrs. Scribner proposed to print the book in America, I stipulated that I should be allowed to rewrite it. They consented, and I began the story with Emily Watson, making her the principal character instead of Hubert Price. Some months after I received a letter from Madam Couperus, offering to translate the English edition into Dutch. I sent her the American edition, and asked her which she would prefer to translate from. Madam Couperus replied that many things in the English edition, which she would like to retain, had been omitted from the American edition, that the hundred or more pages which I had written for the American edition seemed to her equally worthy of retention.

She pointed out that, without the alteration of a sentence, the two versions could be combined. The idea had not occurred to me; I saw, however, that what she proposed was not only feasible but advantageous. I wrote, therefore, giving her the required permission, and thanking her for a suggestion which I should avail myself of when the time came for a new English edition.

The union of the texts was no doubt accomplished by Madam Couperus, without the alteration of a sentence; but no such accomplished editing is possible to me; I am a victim to the disease of rewriting, and the inclusion of the hundred or more pages of new matter written for the American edition led me into a third revision of the story. But no more than in the second has the skeleton, or the attitude of the skeleton been altered in this third version, only flesh and muscle have been added, and, I think, a little life.

Vain Fortune, even in its present form, is probably

not my best book, but it certainly is far from being my worst. But my opinion regarding my own work is of no value; I do not write this Prefatory Note to express it, but to ask my critics and my readers to forget the original *Vain Fortune*, and to read this new book as if it were issued under another title.

G. M.

VAIN FORTUNE

———◆———

I

THE lamp had not been wiped, and the room smelt slightly of paraffin. The old window-curtains, whose harsh green age had not softened, were drawn. The mahogany sideboard, the threadbare carpet, the small horsehair sofa, the gilt mirror, standing on a white marble chimney-piece, said clearly, 'Furnished apartments in a house built about a hundred years ago.' There were piles of newspapers, there were books on the mahogany sideboard and on the horsehair sofa, and on the table there were various manuscripts,— *The Gipsy*, Act I.; *The Gipsy*, Act III., Scenes iii. and iv.

A sheet of foolscap paper, and upon it a long slender hand. The hand traced a few lines of fine, beautiful caligraphy, then it paused, correcting with extreme care what was already written, and in a hesitating, minute way, telling of a brain that delighted in the correction rather than in the creation of form.

The shirt-cuff was frayed and dirty. The coat was thin and shiny. A half-length figure of a man drew out of the massed shadows between the window and sideboard. The red beard caught the light, and the wavy brown hair brightened. Then a look of weariness, of distress, passed over the face, and the man laid down the pen, and, taking some tobacco from a paper, rolled a cigarette. Rising, and leaning forward, he lighted it over the lamp. He was a man of about thirty—six feet, broad-shouldered, well-built, healthy, almost handsome.

The time he spent in dreaming his play amounted to six times, if not ten times, as much as he devoted to trying to write it; and he now lit cigarette after cigarette, abandoning himself to every meditation,—the unpleasantness of life in lodgings, the charm of foreign travel, the beauty of the south, what he would do if his play succeeded. He plunged into calculation of the time it would take him to finish it if he were to sit at home all day, working from seven to ten hours every day. If he could but make up his mind concerning the beginning and the middle of the third act, and about the end, too,—the solution,—he felt sure that, with steady work, the play could be completed in a fortnight. In such reverie and such consideration he lay immersed, oblivious of the present moment; and did not stir from his chair until the postman shook the frail walls with a violent double knock. He hoped for a letter, for a newspaper—either would prove a welcome distraction. The servant's footsteps on the stairs told him the post had brought him something. His heart sank at the thought that it was probably only a bill, and he glanced at all the bills lying one above another on the table.

It was not a bill, nor yet an advertisement, but a copy of a weekly review. He tore it open. An article about himself!

After referring to the deplorable condition of the modern stage, the writer pointed out how dramatic writing has of late years come to be practised entirely by men who have failed in all other branches of literature. Then he drew attention to the fact that signs of weariness and dissatisfaction with the old stale stories, the familiar tricks in bringing about 'striking situations,' were noticeable, not only in the newspaper criticisms of new plays, but also among the better portion of the audience. He admitted, however, that hitherto the attempts made by younger writers in the

3

direction of new subject-matter and new treatment had met with little success. But this, he held, was not a reason for discouragement. Did those who believed in the old formulas imagine that the new formula would be discovered straight away, without failures preliminary? Besides, these attempts were not utterly despicable; at least one play written on the new lines had met with some measure of success, and that play was Mr. Hubert Price's *Divorce*.

'Yes, the fellow is right. The public is ready for a good play: it wasn't when *Divorce* was given. I must finish *The Gipsy*. There are good things in it; that I know. But I wish I could get that third act right. The public will accept a masterpiece, but it will not accept an attempt to write a masterpiece. But this time there'll be no falling off in the last acts. The scene between the gipsy lover and the young lord will fetch 'em.' Taking up the review, Hubert glanced over the article a second time. 'How anxious the fellows are for me to achieve a success! How they believe in me! They desire it more than I do. They believe in me more than I do in myself. They want to applaud me. They are hungry for the masterpiece.'

At that moment his eye was caught by some letters written on blue paper. His face resumed a wearied

4

and hunted expression. 'There's no doubt about it, money I must get somehow. I am running it altogether too fine. There isn't twenty pounds between me and the deep sea.'

* * * * *

He was the son of the Rev. James Price, a Shropshire clergyman. The family was of Welsh extraction, but in Hubert none of the physical characteristics of the Celt appeared. He might have been selected as a typical Anglo-Saxon. The face was long and pale, and he wore a short reddish beard; the eyes were light blue, verging on grey, and they seemed to speak a quiet, steadfast soul. Hubert had always been his mother's favourite, and the scorn of his elder brothers, two rough boys, addicted in early youth to robbing orchards, and later on to gambling and drinking. The elder, after having broken his father's heart with debts and disgraceful living, had gone out to the Cape. News of his death came to the Rectory soon after; but James's death did not turn Henry from his evil courses, and one day his father and mother had to go to London on his account, and they brought him back a hopeless invalid. Hubert was twelve years of age when he followed his brother to the grave.

It was at his brother's funeral that Hubert met for the first time his uncle, Mr. Burnett. Mr. Burnett had spent the greater part of his life in New Zealand, where he had made a large fortune by sheep-farming and investments in land. He had seemed to be greatly taken with his nephew, and for many years it was understood that he would leave him the greater part, if not the whole, of his fortune. But Mr. Burnett had come under the influence of some poor relations, some distant cousins, the Watsons, and had eventually decided to adopt their daughter Emily and leave her his fortune. He did not dare intimate his change of mind to his sister; but the news having reached Mrs. Price in various rumours, she wrote to her brother asking him to confirm or deny these rumours; and when he admitted their truth, Mrs. Price never spoke to him again. She was a determined woman, and the remembrance of the wrong done to her son never left her.

While the other children had been a torment and disgrace, Hubert had been to his parents a consolation and a blessing. They had feared that he too might turn to betting and drink, but he had never shown sign of low tastes. He played no games, nor did he care for terriers or horses; but for books and drawing,

and long country walks. Immediately on hearing of
his disinheritance he had spoken at once of entering a
profession ; and for many months this was the subject
of consideration in the Rectory. Hubert joined in
these discussions willingly, but he could not bring himself to accept the army or the bar. It was indeed
only necessary to look at him to see that neither
soldier's tunic nor lawyer's wig was intended for him ;
and it was nearly as clear that those earnest eyes, so
intelligent and yet so undetermined in their gaze, were
not those of a doctor.

But if his eyes failed to predict his future, his hands
told the story of his life distinctly enough—those long,
white, languid hands, what could they mean but art ?
And very soon Hubert began to draw, evincing some
natural aptitude. Then an artist came into the neighbourhood, the two became friends, and went together
on a long sketching tour. Life in the open air, the
shade of the hedge, the glare of the highway, the
meditation of the field, the languor of the river-
side, the contemplation of wooded horizons, was what
Hubert's pastoral nature was most fitted to enjoy ; and,
for the sake of the life it afforded him, he pursued the
calling of a landscape painter long after he had begun
to feel his desire turning in another direction. When

the landscape on the canvas seemed hopelessly inade-
quate, he laid aside the brush for the pencil, and strove
to interpret the summer fields in verse. From verse he
drifted into the article and the short story, and from
the story into the play. And it was in this last form
that he felt himself strongest, and various were the
dramas and comedies that he dreamed from year's end
to year's end.

While he was in the midst of his period of verse-
writing his mother died, and in the following year, just
as he was working at his stories, he received a telegram
calling him to attend his father's death-bed. When
the old man was laid in the shadow of the weather-
beaten village church, Hubert gathered all his be-
longings and bade farewell for ever to the Shropshire
rectory.

In London Hubert made few friends. There were
some two or three men with whom he was frequently
seen—quiet folk like himself, whose enjoyment con-
sisted in smoking a tranquil pipe in the evening, or
going for long walks in the country. He was one of
those men whose indefiniteness provokes curiosity, and
his friends noticed and wondered why it was that he
was so frequently the theme of their conversation. His
simple, unaffected manners were full of suggestion,

and in his writings there was always an indefinable rainbow-like promise of ultimate achievement. So, long before he had succeeded in writing a play, detached scenes and occasional verses led his friends into gradual belief that he was one from whom big things might be expected. And when the one-act play which they had all so heartily approved of was produced, and every newspaper praised it for its literary quality, the friends took pride in this public vindication of their opinion. After the production of his play people came to see the new author, and every Saturday evening some fifteen or twenty men used to assemble in Hubert's lodgings to drink whisky, smoke cigars, and talk drama. Encouraged by his success, Hubert wrote *Divorce*. He worked unceasingly upon it for more than a year, and when he had written the final scene, he was breaking into his last hundred pounds. The play was refused twice, and then accepted by a theatrical speculator, to whom it seemed to afford opportunity for the exhibition of the talents of a lady he was interested in.

The success of the play was brief. But before it was withdrawn, Hubert had sold the American rights for a handsome sum, and within the next two years he had completed a second play, which he

9

called *An Ebbing Tide.* Some of the critics argued
that it contained scenes as fine as any in *Divorce,*
but it was admitted on all sides that the interest
withered in the later acts. But the failure of the
play did not shake the established belief in Hubert's
genius ; it merely concentrated the admiration of those
interested in the new art upon *Divorce,* the partial
failure of which was now attributed to the acting. If it
had only been played at the Haymarket or the Lyceum,
it could not have failed.

The next three years Hubert wasted in various
æstheticisms. He explained the difference between
the romantic and realistic methods in the reviews ; he
played with a poetic drama to be called *The King of
the Beggars,* and it was not until the close of the third
year that he settled down to definite work. Then all
his energies were concentrated on a new play—*The
Gipsy.* A young woman of Bohemian origin is
suddenly taken with the nostalgia of the tent, and
leaves her husband and her home to wander with those
of her race. He had read portions of this play to
his friends, who at last succeeded in driving Montague Ford, the popular actor-manager, to Hubert's
door ; and after hearing some few scenes he had
offered a couple of hundred pounds in advance of fees

for the completed manuscript. 'But when can I
have the manuscript?' said Ford, as he was about to
leave. 'As soon as I can finish it,' Hubert replied,
looking at him wistfully out of pale blue-grey eyes.
'I could finish it in a month, if I could count on not
being worried by duns or disturbed by friends during
that time.'

Ford looked at Hubert questioningly ; then he said
'I have always noticed that when a fellow wants to
finish a play, the only way to do it is to go away to
the country and leave no address.'

But the country was always so full of pleasure for
him, that he doubted his power to remain indoors with
the temptation of fields and rivers before his eyes, and
he thought that to escape from dunning creditors it
would be sufficient to change his address. So he left
Norfolk Street for the more remote quarter of Fitzroy
Street, where he took a couple of rooms on the second
floor. One of his fellow-lodgers, he soon found, was
Rose Massey, an actress engaged for the performance
of small parts at the Queen's Theatre. The first time
he spoke to her was on the doorstep. She had forgotten her latch-key, and he said, 'Will you allow me
to let you in?' She stepped aside, but did not answer
him. Hubert thought her rude, but her strange eyes

and absent-minded manner had piqued his curiosity, and, having nothing to do that night, he went to the theatre to see her act. She was playing a very small part, and one that was evidently unsuited to her—a part that was in contradiction to her nature; but there was something behind the outer envelope which led him to believe she had real talent, and would make a name for herself when she was given a part that would allow her to reveal what was in her.

In the meantime, Rose had been told that the gentleman she had snubbed in the passage was Mr. Hubert Price, the author of *Divorce*.

'Oh, it was very silly of me,' she said to Annie. 'If I had only known!'

'Lor', he don't mind; he'll be glad enough to speak to you when you meets him again.'

And when they met again on the stairs, Rose nodded familiarly, and Hubert said—

'I went to the Queen's the other night.'

'Did you like the piece?'

'I did not care about the piece; but when you get a wild, passionate part to play, you'll make a hit. The sentimental parts they give you don't suit you.'

A sudden light came into the languid face. 'Yes, I shall do something if I can get a part like that.'

Hubert told her that he was writing a play containing just such a part.

Her eyes brightened again. 'Will you read me the play?' she said, fixing her dark, dreamy eyes on him.

'I shall be very glad. . . . Do you think it won't bore you?' And his wistful grey eyes were full of interrogation.

'No, I'm sure it won't.'

And a few days after she sent Annie with a note, reminding him of his promise to read her what he had written. As she had only a bedroom, the reading had to take place in his sitting-room. He read her the first and second acts. She was all enthusiasm, and begged hard to be allowed to study the part—just to see what she could do with it—just to let him see that he was not mistaken in her. Her interest in his work captivated him, and he couldn't refuse to lend her the manuscript.

II

Rose often came to see Hubert in his rooms. Her manner was disappointing, and he thought he must be mistaken in his first judgment of her talents. But one afternoon she gave him a recitation of the sleep-walking scene in *Macbeth*. It was strange to see this little dark-complexioned, dark-eyed girl, the merest handful of flesh and bone, divest herself at will of her personality, and assume the tragic horror of Lady Macbeth, or the passionate rapture of Juliet detaining her husband-lover on the balcony of her chamber. Hubert watched in wonderment this girl, so weak and languid in her own nature, awaking only to life when she assumed the personality of another. There she lay, her wispy form stretched in his arm-chair, her great dark eyes fixed, her mind at rest, sunk in some inscrutable dream. Her thin hand lay on the arm of the chair: when she woke from her day-dream she burst into irresponsible laughter, or questioned him with petulant curiosity. He looked again: her dark curling hair hung on her swarthy neck, and she was somewhat untidily dressed in blue linen.

'Were you ever in love?' she said suddenly. 'I don't suppose you could be; you are too occupied with your play. I don't know, though; you might be in love, but I don't think that many women would be in love with you . . . You are too good a man, and women don't like good men.'

Hubert laughed, and without a trace of offended vanity in his voice he said, 'I don't profess to be much of a lady-killer.'

'You don't know what I mean,' she said, looking at him fixedly, a maze of half-childish, half-artistic curiosity in her handsome eyes.

Perplexed in his shy, straightford nature, Hubert inquired if she took sugar in her tea. She said she did; stretched her feet to the fire, and lapsed into dream. She was one of the enigmas of Stageland. She supported herself, and went about by herself, looking a poor, lost little thing. She spoke with considerable freedom of language on all subjects, but no one had been able to fix a lover upon her.

'What a part Lady Hayward is! But tell me,—I don't quite catch your meaning in the second act. Is this it?' and starting to her feet, she became in a moment another being. With a gesture, a look, an intonation, she was the woman of the play,—a woman taken by an instinct, long submerged, but which has floated to the surface, and is beginning to command her actions. In another moment she had slipped back into her weary lymphatic nature, at once prematurely old and extravagantly childish. She could not talk of indifferent things; and having asked some strange questions, and laughed loudly, she wished Hubert 'Good-afternoon' in her curious, irresponsible fashion, taking her leave abruptly.

The next two days Hubert devoted entirely to his play. There were things in it which he knew were good, but it was incomplete. Montague Ford would not produce it in its present form. He must put his shoulder to the wheel and get it right; one more push, that was all that was wanted. And he could be heard walking to and fro, up and down, along and across his tiny sitting-room, stopping suddenly to take a note of an idea that had occurred to him.

One day he went to Hampstead Heath. A long walk, he thought, would clear his mind, and he returned home thinking of his play. The sunset still glittering in the skies; the bare trees were beautifully distinct on the blue background of the suburban street,

and at the end of the long perspective, a 'bus and a
hansom could be seen coming towards him. As they
grew larger, his thoughts defined themselves, and the
distressing problem of his fourth act seemed to solve
itself. That very evening he would sketch out a new
dramatic movement around which all the other move
ments of the act would cluster. But at the corner of
Fitzroy Square, within a few yards of No. 17, he was
accosted by a shabbily-dressed man, who inquired if he
were Mr. Price. On being answered in the affirmative,
the shabbily-dressed man said, 'Then I have something
for ye; I have been a-watching for ye for the last three
days, but ye didn't come out; missed yer this morning:
'ere it is;' and he thrust a folded paper into Hubert's
hand.

'What is this?'

'Don't yer know?' he said with a grin; 'Messrs.
Tomkins & Co., Tailors, writ—twenty-two pound odd.'

Hubert made no answer; he put the paper in his
pocket, opened the door quietly, stole up to his room,
and sat down to think. The first thing to do was to
examine into his finances. It was alarming to find that
he was breaking into his last five-pound note. True
that he was close on the end of his play, and when it
was finished he would be able to draw on Ford. But a

summons to appear in the county court could not fail
to do him immense injury. He had heard of avoiding
service, but he knew little of the law, and wondered
what power the service of the writ gave his creditor
over him. His instinct was to escape—hide himself
where they would not be able to find him, and so
obtain time to finish his play. But he owed his landlady
money, and his departure would have to be clandestine.
As he reflected on how many necessaries he might carry
away in a newspaper, he began to feel strangely like a
criminal, and while rolling up a couple of shirts, a few
pairs of socks, and some collars, he paused, his hands
resting on the parcel. He did not seem to know himself, and it was difficult to believe that he really intended to leave the house in this disreputable fashion.
Mechanically he continued to add to his parcel,
thinking all the while that he must go, otherwise his
play would never be written.

He had been working very well for the last few days,
and now he saw his way quite clearly; the inspiration
he had been so long waiting for had come at last, and
he felt sure of his fourth act. At the same time he
wished to conduct himself honestly, even in this distressing situation. Should he tell his landlady the
truth? But the desire to realise his idea was intolerable,

and, yielding as if before an irresistible force, he tied the parcel and prepared to go. At that moment he remembered that he must leave a note for his landlady, and he was more than ever surprised at the naturalness with which lying phrases came into his head. But when it came to committing them to paper, he found he could not tell an absolute lie, and he wrote a simple little note to the effect that he had been called away on urgent business, and hoped to return in about a week.

He descended the stairs softly. Mrs. Wilson's sitting-room opened on to the passage; she might step out at any moment, and intercept his exit. He had nearly reached the last flight when he remembered that he had forgotten his manuscripts. His flesh turned cold, his heart stood still. There was nothing for it but to ascend those creaking stairs again. His already heavily encumbered pockets could not be persuaded to receive more than a small portion of the manuscripts. He gathered them in his hand, and prepared to re-descend the perilous stairs. He walked as lightly as possible, dreading that every creak would bring Mrs. Wilson from her parlour. A few more steps, and he would be in the passage. A smell of dust, sounds of children crying, children talking in the kitchen! A few more steps, and, with his eyes on the parlour door,

Hubert had reached the rug at the foot of the stairs. He hastened along the passage. Mrs. Wilson was a moment too late. His hand was on the street-door when she appeared at the door of her parlour.

'Mr. Price, I want to speak to you before you go out. There has——'

'I can't wait—running to catch a train. You'll find a letter on my table. It will explain.'

Hubert slipped out, closed the door, and ran down the street, and it was not until he had put two or three streets between him and Fitzroy Street that he relaxed his pace, and could look behind him without dreading to feel the hand of the 'writter' upon his shoulder.

III

THEN he wandered, not knowing where he was going, still in the sensation of his escape, a little amused, and yet with a shadow of fear upon his soul, for he grew more and more conscious of the fact that he was homeless, if not quite penniless. Suddenly he stopped walking. Night was thickening in the street, and he had to decide where he would sleep. He could not afford to pay more than five or six shillings a week for a room, and he thought of Holloway, as being a neighbourhood where creditors would not be able to find him. So he retraced his steps, and, tired and footsore, entered the Tottenham Court Road by the Oxford Street end.

There the omnibuses stopped. A conductor shouted for fares, with the light of the public-house lamps on his open mouth. There was smell of mud, of damp clothes, of bad tobacco, and where the lights of the costermongers' barrows broke across the footway the picture was of a group of three coarse, loud-voiced girls, followed by boys. There were fish shops, cheap Italian restaurants, and the long lines of low houses vanished in crapulent night. The characteristics of the Tottenham Court Road impressed themselves on Hubert's mind, and he thought how he would have to bear for at least three weeks with all the grime of its poverty. It would take about that time to finish his play, and the neighbourhood would suit his purpose excellently well. So long as he did not pass beyond it he ran little risk of discovery, and to secure himself against friends and foes he penetrated farther northward, not stopping till he reached the confines of Holloway.

Then a little dim street caught his eye, and he knocked at the door òf the first house exhibiting a card in the, parlour window. But they did not let their bedroom under seven shillings, and this seemed to Hubert to be an extravagant price. He tried farther on, and at last found a clean room for six shillings. Having no luggage, he paid a week's rent in advance, and the landlady promised to get him a small table, on which he could write, a small table that would fit in somewhere near the window. She asked him when he would like to be called, and put the candlestick on the chair. Hubert looked round the room, and a moment sufficed to complete the survey. It was about seven feet long. The lower half of the window was curtained by a piece of muslin hardly bigger than a good-sized pocket-handkerchief; to do anything in this room except to lie in bed seemed difficult, and Hubert sat down on the bed and emptied out his pockets. He had just four pounds, and the calculation how long he could live on such a sum took him some time. His breakfast, whether he had it at home or in the coffee-house, would cost him at least fourpence. He thought he would be able to obtain a fairly good dinner in one of the little Italian restaurants for ninepence. His tea would cost the same as his breakfast. To these sums he must add twopence for tobacco and a penny for an evening paper—impossible to do without tobacco, and he must know what was going on in the world. He could therefore live for one shilling and eightpence a day—eleven shillings a week—to which he would have to add six shillings a week for rent, altogether seventeen shillings a week. He really did not see how he could do it cheaper. Four times seventeen are sixty-eight; sixty-eight shillings for a month of life, and he had eighty shillings—twelve shillings for incidental expenses; and out of that twelve shillings he must buy a shirt, a sponge, and a tooth brush, and when they were bought there would be very little left. He must finish his play under the month. Nothing could be clearer than that.

Next morning he asked the landlady to let him have a cup of tea and some bread and butter, and he ate as much bread as he could, to save himself from being hungry in the middle of the day. He began work immediately, and continued until seven, and feeling then somewhat light-headed, but satisfied with himself, went to the nearest Italian restaurant. The food was better than he expected; but he spent twopence more than he had intended, so, to accustom himself to a life of strict measure and discipline, he determined to forego his tea that evening. And so he lived and worked until the end of the week.

But the situation he had counted on to complete his fourth act had proved almost impracticable in the working out; he laboured on, however, and at the end of the tenth day at least one scene satisfied him. He read it over slowly, carefully, thought about it, decided that it was excellent, and lay down on his bed to consider it. At that moment it struck him that he had better calculate how much he had spent in the last ten days. He gathered himself into a sitting posture and counted his money; he had spent thirty shillings, and at that rate his money would not hold out till the end of the month. He must reduce his expenditure; but how? Impossible to find a room where he could live more cheaply than in the one he had got, and it is not easy to dine in London on less than ninepence. Only the poor can live cheaply. He pressed his hands to his face. His head seemed like splitting, and his monetary difficulty, united with his literary difficulties, produced a momentary insanity. Work that morning was impossible, so he went out to study the eating-houses of the neighbourhood. He must find one where he could dine for sixpence. Or he might buy a pound of cooked beef and take it home with him in a paper bag; but that would seem an almost intolerable imprisonment in his little room. He could go to a public-house and dine off a sausage and potato. But at that moment his attention was caught by black letters on a dun, yellowish ground: 'Lockhart's Cocoa Rooms.' Not having breakfasted, he decided to have a cup of cocoa and a roll.

It was a large, barn-like place, the walls covered with a coat of grey-blue paint. Under the window there was a zinc counter, with zinc urns always steaming, emiting odours of tea, coffee, and cocoa. The seats were like those which give a garden-like appearance to the tops of some omnibuses. Each was made to hold

two persons, and the table between them was large
enough for four plates and four pairs of hands. A few
hollow-chested men, the pale vagrants of civilisation,
drowsed in the corners. They had been hunted
through the night by the policeman, and had come in
for something hot. Hubert noted the worn frock-coats,
and the miserable arms coming out of shirtless sleeves.
One looked up inquiringly, and Hubert thought how
slight had become the line that divided him from the
outcast. A serving-maid collected the plates, knives
and forks, when the customers left, and carried them
back to the great zinc counter.

Impressed by his appearance, she brought him what
he had ordered and took the money for it, although the
custom of the place was for the customer to pay for
food at the counter and carry it himself to the table at
which he chose to eat. Hubert learnt that there was
no set dinner, but there was a beef-steak pudding at
one, price fourpence, a penny potatoes, a penny bread.
So by dining at Lockhart's he would be able to cut
down his daily expense by at least twopence; that
would extend the time to finish his play by nearly a
week. And if his appetite were not keen, he could
assuage it with a penny plum pudding; or he could
take a middle course, making his dinner off a sausage

and mashed potatoes. The room was clean, well lighted, and airy; he could read his paper there, and forget his troubles in the observation of character. He even made friends. An old wizen creature, who had been a prize-fighter, told him of his triumphs. If he hadn't broke his hand on somebody's nose he'd have been champion light-weight of England. 'And to think that I have come to this,' he added emphatically. 'Even them boys knock me about now, and 'alf a century ago I could 'ave cleared the bloomin' place.' There was a merry little waif from the circus who loved to come and sit with Hubert. She had been a rider, she said, but had broken her leg on one occasion, and cut her head all open on another, and had ended by running away with some one who had deserted her. 'So here I am,' she remarked, with a burst of laughter, 'talking to you. Did you never hear of Dolly Dayrell?' Hubert confessed that he had not. 'Why,' she said, 'I thought every one had.'

About eight o'clock in the evening, the table near the stairs was generally occupied by flower-girls, dressed in dingy clothes, and brightly feathered hats. They placed their empty baskets on the floor, and shouted at their companions—men who sold newspapers, boot-laces, and cheap toys. About nine the boys came in, the boys who used to push the old prize-fighter about, and Hubert soon began to perceive how representative they were of all vices—gambling, theft, idleness, and cruelty were visible in their faces. They were led by a Jew boy who sold penny jewellery at the corner of Oxford Street, and they generally made for the tables at the end of the room, for there, unless custom was slack indeed, they could defeat the vigilance of the serving-maid and play at nap at their ease. The tray of penny jewellery was placed at the corner of a table, and a small boy set to watch over it. His duty was also to shuffle his feet when the servant-maid approached, and a precious drubbing he got if he failed to shuffle them loud enough. The ' 'ot un,' as he was nicknamed, always had a pack of cards in his pocket, and to annex everything left on the tables he considered to be his privilege. One day, when he was asked how he came by the fine carnation in his buttonhole, he said it was a present from Sally, neglecting to add that he had told the child to steal it from a basket which a flower-girl had just put down.

Hubert hated this boy, and once could not resist boxing his ears. The ' 'ot un ' writhed easily out of his reach, and then assailed him with foul language, and so loud were his words that they awoke the innocent

cause of the quarrel, a weak, sickly-looking man, with pale blue eyes and a blonde beard. Hubert had protected him before now against the brutality of the boys, who, when they were not playing nap, divided their pleasantries between him and the decrepit prize-fighter. He came in about nine, took a cup of coffee from the counter, and settled himself for a snooze. The boys knew this, and it was their amusement to keep him awake by pelting him with egg-shells and other missiles. Hubert noticed that he had always with him a red handkerchief full of some sort of loose rubbish, which the boys gathered when it fell about the floor, or purloined from the handkerchief when they judged that the owner was sufficiently fast asleep. Hubert now saw that the handkerchief was filled with bits of coloured chalk, and guessed that the man must be a pavement artist.

'A dirty, hignominious lot, them boys is,' said the artist, fixing his pale, melancholy eyes on Hubert; 'bad manners, no eddication, and, above all, no respect.'

'They are an unmannerly lot—that Jew boy especially. I don't think there's a vice he hasn't got.'

The artist stared at Hubert a long time in silence. A thought seemed to be stirring in his mind.

'I'm speaking, I can see, to a man of eddication.

I'm a fust-rate judge of character, though I be but a pavement artist; but a picture's none the less a picture, no matter where it is drawn. That's true, ain't it?'

'Quite true. A horse is a horse, and an ass is an ass, no matter what stable you put them into.'

The artist laughed a guttural laugh, and, fixing his pale blue porcelain eyes on Hubert, he said—

'Yes; see I made no bloomin' error when I said you was a man of eddication. A literary gent, I should think. In the reporting line, most like. Down in the luck like myself. What was it—drink? Got the chuck?'

'No,' said Hubert, 'never touch it. Out of work.'

' No offence, master, we're all mortal, we is all weak, and in misfortune we goes to it. It was them boys that drove me to it.'

' How was that?'

'They was always round my show; no getting rid of them, and their remarks created a disturbance; the perlice said he wouldn't 'ave it, and when the perlice won't 'ave it, what's a poor man to do? They are that hignorant. But what's the use of talking of it, it only riles me.' The blue-eyed man lay back in his seat, and his head sank on his chest. He looked as if he were going to sleep again, but on Hubert's asking him to explain his troubles, he leaned across the table.

' Well, I 'll tell yer. Yer be an eddicated man, and
I likes to talk to them that 'as 'ad an eddication. Yer
says, and werry truly, just now, that changing the stable
don't change an 'orse into a hass, or a hass into an 'orse.
That is werry true, most true, none but a eddicated
man could 'ave made that 'ere hobservation. I likes
yer for it. Give us yer 'and. The public just thinks
too much of the stable, and not enough of what 's
inside. Leastways that 's my experience of the public,
and I 'ave been a-catering for the public ever since I
was a growing lad—sides of bacon, ships on fire, good
old ship on fire. . . . I knows the public. Yer don't
follow me ? '

' Not quite.'

' A moment, and I 'll explain. You 'll admit there 's
no blooming reason except the public's blooming
hignorance why a man shouldn't do as good a picture
on the pavement as on a piece of canvas, provided he
'ave the blooming genius. There is no doubt that with
them 'ere chalks and a nice smooth stone that Raphael
—I 'ave been to the National Gallery and 'ave studied
'is work, and werry fine some of it is, although I don't
altogether hold—but that 's another matter. What was
I a-saying of? I remember,—that with them 'ere
chalks, and a nice smooth stone, there 's no reason why

a masterpiece shouldn't be done. That's right, ain't it? I ask you, as a man of eddication, to say if that ain't right; as a representative of the Press, I asks you to say.' Hubert nodded, and the pale-eyed man continued. 'Well, that's what the public won't see, can't see. Raphael, says I, could 'ave done a masterpiece with them 'ere chalks and a nice smooth stone. But do yer think 'e 'd 'ave been allowed? Do yer think the perlice would 'ave stood it? Do yer think the public would 'ave stood him doing masterpieces on the pavement? I'd give 'im just one afternoon. Them boys would 'ave got 'im into trouble, just as they did me. Raphael would 'ave been told to wipe them out just as I was.'

The conversation paused; and, half amused, half frightened, Hubert considered the pale vague face, and he was struck by the scattered look of aspiration that wandered in the pale blue eyes.

'I'll tell you,' said the man, growing more excited, and leaning further across the table; 'I'll tell you, because I knows you for an eddicated man, and won't blab. S'pose yer thinks, like the rest of the world, that the chaps wot smears, for it ain't drawing, the pavement with bits of bacon, a ship on fire, and the regulation oysters, does them out of their own 'eads?' Hubert nodded. 'I'm not surprised that you do, all the world do, and the public chucks down its coppers to the poor hartist; but 'e aint no hartist, no more than is them 'ere boys that did for my show.' Leaning still further forward, he lowered his voice to a whisper. 'They learns it all by 'art; there is schools for the teaching of it down in Whitechapel. They can just do what they learns by 'art, not one one of them could draw that 'ere chair or table from natur'; but I could. I 'ave an original talent. It was a long time afore I found out it was there,' he said, tapping his forehead; 'but it is there,' he said, fixing his eyes on Hubert, 'and when it is there they can't take it away—I mean my mates—though they do laugh at my ideas. They call me "the genius," for they don't believe in me, but I believe in myself, and they laughs best that laughs last. . . . I don't know,' he said, looking round him, his eyes full of reverie, 'that the public liked my fancy landscapes better than the ship on fire, but I said the public will come to them in time, and I continued my fancy landscapes. But one day in Trafalgar Square it came on to rain very 'eavy, and I went for shelter into the National Gallery. It was my fust visit, and I was struck all of a 'cap, and ever since I can 'ardly bring myself to go on with the drudgery of the piece of bacon, and the piece of cheese, with the mouse nibbling at it. And ever since my 'ead 'as been filled with other things, though for a long time I could not make exactly out what. I 'ave 'eard that that is always the case with men that 'as an idea—daresay you 'ave found it so yourself. So in my spare time I goes to the National to think it out, and in studying the pictures there I got wery interested in a chap called Hetty, and 'e do paint the female form divine. I says to myself, Why not go in for lovely woman ? the public may not care for fancy landscapes, but the public allus likes a lovely woman, and, as well as being popular, lovely woman is 'igh 'art. So, after dinner hour, I sets to work, and sketches in a blue sea with three bathers, and two boxes, with the 'orse's head looking out from behind one of the boxes. For a fust attempt at the nude, I assure you—it ain't my way to blow my own trumpet, but I can say that the crowd that 'ere picture did draw was bigger than any that 'ad assembled about the bits o' bacon and ship-a-fire of all the other coves. 'Ad I been let alone, I should 'ave made my fortune, but the crowd was so big and the curiosity so great that it took the perlice all their time to keep the pavement from being blocked. It wasn't that the public didn't like it enough, it was that the public liked it too much, that was the reason of my misfortune.'

34

'What do you mean?' said Hubert.

'Well, yer see them boys was a-hawking their cheap toys in the neighbourhood, and when they got wind of my success they comes round to see, and they remains on account of the crowd. Pockets was picked, I don't say they wasn't, and the perlice turned rusty, and then a pious old gent comes along, and 'earing the remarks of them boys, which I admit wasn't nice, complains to the hauthorities, and I was put down! Now, what I wants to know is why my art should be made to suffer for the beastly-mindedness of them 'ere boys.'

Hubert admitted that there seemed to be an injustice somewhere, and asked the artist if he had never tried again.

'Try again? Should think I did. When once a man 'as tasted of 'igh art, he can't keep his blooming fingers out of it. It was impossible after the success of my bathers to go back to the bacon, so I thought I would circumvent the hauthorities. I goes to the National Gallery, makes a sketch, 'ere it is,' and after some fumbling in his breast pocket, he produced a greasy piece of paper, which he handed to Hubert. 'S'pose yer know the picture?' Hubert admitted that he did not. 'Well, that is a drawing from Gainsborough's celebrated picture of Medora a-washing of

35

her feet . . . But the perlice wouldn't 'ave it any more than my original, 'e said it was worse than the bathers at Margaret, and when I told the hignorant brute wot it was, 'e said he wanted no hargument, that 'e wouldn't 'ave it.'

Hubert had noticed, during the latter part of the narrative, a look of dubious cunning twinkling in the pale eyes; but now this look died away, and the eyes resumed their habitual look of vague reverie.

'I've been 'ad up before the Beak: from him I expected more enlightenment, but he, too, said 'e wouldn't 'ave it, and I got a month. But I'll beat them yet, the public is on my side, and if it worn't for them 'ere boys, I'd say that the public could be helevated. They calls me "the genius," and they is right.' Then something seemed to go out like a flame, the face grew dim, and changed expression. 'It is 'ere all right,' he said, no longer addressing Hubert, but speaking to himself, 'and since it is there, it must come out.'

IV .

HUBERT at last found himself obliged to write to Ford
for an advance of money. But Ford replied that he
would advance money only on the delivery of the
completed manuscript. And the whole of one night,
in a room hardly eight feet long, sitting on his bed,
he strove to complete the fourth and fifth acts. But
under the pressure of such necessity ideas died within
him. And all through the night, and even when the
little window, curtained with a bit of muslin hardly
bigger than a pocket-handkerchief, had grown white
with dawn, he sat gazing at the sheet of paper, his
brain on fire, unable to think. Laying his pen down
in despair, he thought of the thousands who would
come to his aid if they only knew—if they only knew !
And soon after he heard life beginning again in the
little brick street. He felt that his brain was giving
way, that if he did not find change, whatever it was,
he must surely run raving mad. He had had enough
of England, and would leave it for America, Australia

—anywhere. He wanted change. The present was unendurable. How would he get to America? Perhaps a clerkship on board one of the great steamships might be obtained.

The human animal in extreme misery becomes self-reliant, and Hubert hardly thought of making application to his uncle. The last time he had applied for help his letter had remained unanswered, and he now felt that he must make his own living or die. And, quite indifferent as to what might befall him, he walked next day to the Victoria Docks. He did not know where or how to apply for work, and he tired himself in fruitless endeavour. At last he felt he could strive with fate no longer, and wandered mile after mile, amused and forgetful of his own misery in the spectacle of the river—the rose sky, the long perspectives, the houses and warehouses showing in fine outline, and then the wonderful blue night gathering in the forest of masts and rigging. He was admirably patient. There was . no fretfulness in his soul, nor did he rail against the world's injustice, but took his misfortunes with sweet gentleness.

He slept in a public-house, and next day resumed his idle search for employment. The weather was mild and beautiful, his wants were simple, a cup of coffee and a roll, a couple of sausages, and the day passed in a sort of morose and passionless contemplation. He thought of everything and nothing, least of all of how he should find money for the morrow. When the day came, and the penny to buy a cup of coffee was wanting, he quite naturally, without giving it a second thought, engaged himself as a labourer, and worked all day carrying sacks of grain out of a vessel's hold. For a large part of his nature was patient and simple, docile as an animal's. There was in him so much that was rudimentary, that in accepting this burden of physical toil he was acting not in contradiction to, but in full and perfect harmony with, his true nature.

But at the end of a week his health began to give way, and, like a man after a violent debauch, he thought of returning to a more normal existence. He had left the manuscript of his unfortunate play in the North. Had they destroyed it? The involuntary fear of the writer for his child made him smile. What did it matter? Clearly the first thing to do would be to write to the editor of *The Cosmopolitan*, and ask if he could find him some employment, something certain; writing occasional articles for newspapers, that he couldn't do.

Hubert had saved twelve shillings. He would therefore be able to pay his landlady : he smiled—one of
his landladies ! The earlier debt was now hopelessly
out of his reach, and seemed to represent a social
plane from which he had for ever fallen. If he had succeeded in getting that play right, what a difference it
would have made ! He would have been able to do a
number of things he had never done, things which he
had always desired to do. He had desired above all
to travel—to see France and Italy ; to linger, to muse
in the shadows of the world's past ; and after this he
had desired marriage, an English wife, an English
home, beautiful children, leisure, the society of friends.
A successful play would have given him all these
things, and now his dream must remain for ever unrealised by him. He had sunk out of sight and hearing of such life.

Rose was another ; she might sink as he had sunk ;
she might never find the opportunity of realising her
desire. How well she would have played that part !
He knew what was in her. And now ! What did his
failure to write that play condemn him to ? Heaven
only knows, he did not wish to think. Strange, was it
not strange ? . . . A man of genius—many believed
him a genius—and yet he was incapable of earning his

daily bread otherwise than by doing the work of a navvy. Even that he could not do well, society had softened his muscles and effeminised his constitution. Indeed, he did not know what life fate had willed him for. He seemed to be out of place everywhere. His best chance was to try to obtain a clerkship. The editor of *The Cosmopolitan* might be able to do that for him; if he could not, far better it would be to leave a world in which he was *out of place*, and through no fault of his own—that was the hard part of it. Hard part! Nonsense! What does Fate know of our little rights and wrongs—or care? Her intentions are inscrutable; she watches us come and go, and gives no sign. Prayers are vain. The good man is punished, and the wicked is sent on his way rejoicing.

In such mournful thought, his clothes stained and torn, with all the traces of a week's toil in the docks upon them, Hubert made his way round St. Paul's and across Holborn. As he was about to cross into Oxford Street, he heard some one accost him,—

'Oh, Mr. Price, is that you?' It was Rose. 'Where have you been all this time?'

She seemed so strange, so small, and so much alone in the great thoroughfare, that Hubert forgot all his own troubles in a sudden interest in this little mite.

'Where have you been hiding yourself? . . . It is lucky I met you. Don't you know that Ford has decided to revive *Divorce* ? '

' You don't mean it ! '

'Yes; Ford said that the last acts of *The Gipsy* were not satisfactorily worked out, and as there was something wrong with that Hamilton Brown's piece, he has decided to revive *Divorce*. He says it never was properly played . . . he thinks he'll make a hit in the husband's part, and I daresay he will. But I have been unfortunate again; I wanted the part of the adventuress. I really could play it. I don't look it, I know . . . I have no weight, but I could play it for all that. The public mightn't see me in it at first, but in five minutes they would.'

' And what part has he cast you for—the young girl ? '

' Of course ; there's no other part. He says I look it; but what's the good of looking it when you don't feel it? If he had cast me for Mrs. Barrington, I should have had just the five minutes in the second act that I have been waiting for so long, and I should have just wiped Miss Osborne out, acted her off the stage . . . I know I should ; you needn't believe it if don't like, but I know I should.'

Hubert wondered how any one could feel so sure of herself, and then he said, 'Yes, I think you could do just what you say. . . . How do you think Miss Osborne will play the part?'

'She'll be correct enough; she'll miss nothing, and yet somehow she'll miss the whole thing. But you must go at once to Ford. He was saying only this morning that if you didn't turn up soon, he'd have to give up the idea.'

'I can't go and see him to-night. You see what a state I'm in.'

'You're rather dusty; where have you been? what have you been doing?'

'I've been down at the dock. . . . I thought of going to America.'

'Well, we'll talk about that another time. It doesn't matter if you are a bit dusty and worn-out-looking. Now that he's going to revive your play, he'll let you have some money. You might get a new hat, though. I don't know how much they cost, but I've five shillings; can you get one for that?'

Hubert thanked her.

'But you are not offended?'

'Offended, my dear Rose! I shall be able to manage. I'll get a brush up somewhere.'

'That's all right. Now I'm going to jump into that 'bus,' and she signed with her parasol to the conductor. 'Mind you see Ford to-night,' she cried ; and a moment after he saw a small space of blue back seated against one of the windows.

V

THERE was much prophecy abroad. Stiggins' words, 'The piece never did, and never will draw money,' were evidently present in everybody's mind. They were visible in Ford's face, and more than once Hubert expected to hear that—on account of severe indisposition—Mr. Montague Ford has been obliged to indefinitely postpone his contemplated revival of Mr. Hubert Price's play *Divorce*. But, besides the apprehension that Stiggins' unfavourable opinion of his enterprise had engendered in him, Ford was obviously provoked by Hubert's reluctance to execute the alterations he had suggested. Night after night, sometimes until six in the morning, Hubert. sat up considering them. Thanks to Ford's timely advance he was back in his old rooms in Fitzroy Street. All was as it had been. He was working at his play every evening, waiting for Rose's footsteps on the stairs. And yet a change had come into his life ! He believed now that his feet were set on the way to fortune—that he would soon be happy.

He stared at the bright flame of the lamp, he listened to the silence. The clock chimed sharply, and the windows were growing grey. Hubert had begun to drowse in his chair; but he had promised to rewrite the young girl's part, Ford having definitely refused to intrust Rose with the part of the adventuress. He was sorry for this. He believed that Rose had not only talent, but genius. Besides, they were friends, neighbours; he would like to give her a chance of distinguishing herself—the chance which she was seeking. All the time he could not but realise that, however he might accentuate and characterise the part of the sentimental girl, Rose would not be able to do much with it. To bring out her special powers something strange, wild, or tragic was required. But of what use thinking of what was not to be? Having made some alterations and additions he folded his papers up, and addressed them to Miss Massey. He wrote on a piece of paper that they were to be given to her at once, and that he was to be called at ten. There was a rehearsal at twelve.

On the night of the first performance, Hubert asked Rose to dine in his rooms. Mr. Wilson proposed that they should have a roast chicken, and Annie was sent to fetch a bottle of champagne from the grocer's. Annie had been given a ticket for the pit. Mrs. Wilson was going to the upper boxes. Annie said,—

'Why, you look as if you was going to a funeral, and not to a play. Why don't ye laugh?'

In truth, Hubert and Rose were a little silent. Rose was thinking how she could say certain lines. She had said them right once at rehearsal, but had not since been able to reproduce to her satisfaction a certain effect of voice. Hubert was too nervous to talk. There was nothing in his mind but 'Will the piece succeed? What shall I do if it fails?' He could give heed to nothing but himself, all the world seemed blotted out, and he suffered the pain of excessive self-concentration. Rose, on the other hand, had lost sight of herself, and existed almost unconsciously in the soul of another being. She was sometimes like a hypnotised spectator watching with foolish, involuntary curiosity the actions of one whom she had been bidden to watch. Then a little cloud would gather over her eyes, and then this other being would rise as if out of her very entrails and recreate her, fashioning her to its own image and likeness.

She did not answer when she was spoken to, and

when the question was repeated, she awoke with a little start. Dinner was eaten in morbid silence, with painful and fitful efforts to appear interested in each other. Walking to the theatre, they once took the wrong turning and had to ask the way. At the stage door they smiled painfully, nodded, glad to part. Hubert went up to Montague Ford's room. He found the comedian on a low stool, seated before a low table covered with brushes and cosmetics, in front of a triple glass.

'My dear friend, do not trouble me now. I am thinking of my part.'

Hubert turned to go.

'Stay a moment,' cried the actor. 'You know when the husband meets the wife he has divorced?'

Hubert remembered the moment referred to, and, with anxious, doubting eyes, the comedian sought from the author justification for some intonations and gestures which seemed to him to form part and parcel of the nature of the man whose drunkenness he had so admirably depicted on his face.

'"*This is most unfortunate, very unlucky—very, my dear Louisa ; but——*"

'"*I am no longer obliged to bear with your insults ; I can now defend myself against you.*"

"IN THE THIRD ROW HARDING STOOD TALKING TO A YOUNG MAN."

'Now, is that your idea of the scene?'

A pained look came upon Hubert's face. 'Don't question me now, my dear fellow. I cannot fix my attention. I can see, however, that your make-up is capital—you are the man himself.'

The actor was satisfied, and in his satisfaction he said, 'I think it will be all right, old chap.'

Hubert hoped to reach his box without meeting critics or authors. The serving-maids bowed and smiled,—he was the author of the play. 'They'll think still more of me if the notices are right,' he thought, as he hurried upstairs, and from behind the curtain of his box he peeped down and counted the critics who edged their way down the stalls. Harding stood in the third row talking to a young man. He said, 'You mean the woman with the black hair piled into a point, and fastened with a steel circlet. A face of sheep-like sensuality. Red lips and a round receding chin. A large bosom, and two thin arms showing beneath the opera cloak, which she has not yet thrown from her shoulders. I do not know her—*une laideur attirante*. Many a man might be interested in her. But do you see the woman in the stage-box? You would not believe it, but she is sixty, and has only just begun to speak of herself as an

old woman. She kept her figure, and had an admirer
when she was fifty-eight.'

'What has become of him ?'

'They quarrelled; two years ago he told her he
hoped never to see her ugly old face again. And that
delicate little creature in the box next to her—that pale
diaphanous face?'

'With a young man hanging over her whispering in
her ear?'

'Yes. She hates the theatre; it gives her neuralgia;
but she attends all the first nights because her one passion is to be made love to in public. If her admirer
did not hang over her in front of the box just as that
man is doing, she would not tolerate him for a week.'

At that moment the conversation was interrupted by
a new-comer, who asked if he had seen the play when
it was first produced.

'Yes,' said Harding; 'I did.' And he continued
his search for acquaintances amid white rows of female
backs, necks, and half-seen profiles—amid the black
cloth shoulders cut sharply upon the illumined curtain.

'And what do you think of it? Do you think it
will succeed this time?'

'Ford will create an impression in the part; but I
don't think the piece will run.'

'And why? Because the public is too stupid?'

'Partly, and partly because Price is only an inten-
tionist. He cannot carry an idea quite through.'

'Are you going to write about it?'

'I may.'

'And what will you say?'

'Oh, most interesting things to be said. Let's take
the case of Hubert Price . . . Ah, there, the curtain is
going up.'

The curtain rolled slowly up, and in a small country
drawing-room, in very simple but very pointedly written
dialogue, the story of Mrs. Holmes' domestic misfortunes was gradually unfolded. It appeared that she
had flirted with Captain Grey; he had written her
some compromising letters, and she had once been to
his rooms alone. So the Court had pronounced a decree
nisi. But Mrs. Holmes had not been unfaithful to her
husband. She had flirted with Captain Grey because
her husband's attentions to a certain Mrs. Barrington
had maddened her, and in her jealous rage had written
foolish letters, and been to see Captain Grey.

Hubert noticed that folk were still asking for their
seats, and pushing down the very rows in which the
most influential critics were sitting. They exchanged
a salutation with their friends in the dress-circle, and,

when they were seated, looked around, making observations regarding the appearance of the house; and
all˙ the while the actors were speaking. Hubert
trembled with fear and rage. Would these people
never give their attention to the stage? If they had
been sitting by him, he could have struck them. Then
a line turned into nonsense by the actress who played
Mrs. Holmes was a lancinating pain; and the actor
who played Captain Grey, played so slowly that Hubert
could hardly refrain from calling from his box. He
looked round the theatre, noticing the indifferent faces
of the critics, and the women's shoulders seemed to
him especially vacuous and imbecile.

The principal scene of the second act was between
Mrs. Holmes and the man who had divorced her. He
has been driven to drink by the vile behaviour of his
second wife; he is ruined in health and in pocket, and
has come to the woman he wronged to beg forgiveness;
he knows she has learnt to love Captain Grey, but will
not marry him, because she believes that once married
always married. There is only one thing he can do to
repair the wrong he has done—he will commit suicide,
and so enable her to marry the man she loves. He
tells her that he has bought the pistol to do it with,
and the words, 'Not here! not here!' escape from

her; and he answers, 'No, not here, but in a cab. I've got one at the door.' He goes out; Captain Grey enters, and Mrs. Holmes begs him to save her husband. While they are discussing how this is to be done, he re-enters, saying that his conscience smote him as he was going to pull the trigger. Will she forgive him? If she won't, he must make an end of himself. She says she will.

In the third act Hubert had attempted to paint Mr. Holmes' vain efforts to reform his life. But the constant presence of Captain Grey in the household, his attempts to win Mrs. Holmes from her husband, and the drunken husband's amours with the servant-maid disgusted rather than horrified. In the fourth act the wretched husband admits that his reformation is impossible, and that, although he has no courage to commit suicide and set his wife free, he will return to his evil courses; they will sooner or later make an end of him. The slowness and deadly gravity with which Ford took this scene rendered it intolerable; and, notwithstanding the beauty of the conclusion, when the deserted wife, in the silence of her drawing-room, reads again Captain Grey's letter, telling her that he has left England for ever, and with another, the success of the play was left in doubt, and the audience filed out, talking, chattering, arguing, wondering what the public verdict would be.

To avoid commiseration of heartless friends and the triumphant glances of literary enemies, Hubert passed through the door leading on to the stage. Scene-shifters were brutally pushing away what remained of his play; and the presence of Hamilton Brown, the dramatic author, talking to Ford, was at that moment particularly disagreeable. On catching sight of Hubert, Brown ran to him, shook him by the hand, and murmured some discreet congratulations. He preferred the piece, however, as it had been originally written, and suggested to Ford the advisability of returning to the first text. Then Ford went upstairs to take his paint off, and Hubert walked about the stage with Brown. Brown's insincerity was sufficiently transparent; but men in Hubert's position catch at straws, and he soon began to believe that the attitude of the public towards his play was not so unfavourable as he had imagined.

Hubert tried to summon up a smile for the stage-door keeper, who, he feared, had heard that the piece had failed, and then the moment they got outside he begged Rose to tell him the exact truth. She assured him that Ford had said that he had always counted on a certain amount of opposition; but that he believed that the general public, being more free of prejudice and less sophisticated, would be impressed by the simple humanity of the play. The conversation paused, and at the end of an irritating silence he said, 'You were excellent, as good as any one could be in a part that did not suit them. Ah, if he had cast you for the adventuress, how you would have played it! . . .'

'I'm so glad you are pleased. I hope my notices will be good. Do you think they will?'

'Yes, your notices will be all right,' he answered, with a sigh.

'And your notices will be all right too. No one can say what is going to succeed. There was a call after each of the last three acts. . . . I don't see how a piece could go better. It is the suspense. . . .'

'Ah, yes, the suspense!'

They lingered on the landing, and Hubert said, 'Won't you come in for a moment?' She followed him into the room. His calm face, usually a perfect picture of repose and self-possession, betrayed his emotion by a certain blankness in the eyes, certain contractions in the skin of the forehead. 'I'm afraid,' he said, 'there's no hope.'

'Oh, you mustn't say that!' she replied. 'I think it

went very well indeed. . . . I know I did nothing with the young girl. I oughtn't to have undertaken the part.' .

'You were excellent. If we only get some good notices. If we don't, I shall never get another play of mine acted.' He looked at her imploringly, thirsting for a woman's sympathy. But the little girl was thinking of certain effects which she would have made, and which the actress who had played the adventuress had failed to make.

' I watched her all the time,' she said, 'following every line, saying all the time, "Oh yes, that's all very nice and very proper, my young woman; but it's not it; no, not at all—not within a hundred miles of it." I don't think she ever really touched the part—do you?' Hubert did not answer, and a quiver of distraction ran throught the muscles of her face.

' Why don't you answer me ? '

'I can't answer you,' he said abruptly. Then remembering, he added, ' Forgive me; I can think of nothing now.' He hid his face in his hands, and sobbed twice—two heavy, choking sobs, pregnant with the weight of anguish lying on his heart.

Seeing how much he suffered, she laid her hand on his shoulder. 'I am very sorry; I wish I could help you. I know how it tears the heart when one cannot get out what one has in one's brain.'

Her artistic appreciation of his suffering only jarred him the more. What he longed for was some kind, simple-hearted woman who would say, 'Never mind, dear; the play was perfectly right, only they did not understand it; I love you better than ever.' But Rose could not give him the sympathy he wanted; and to be alone was almost a relief. He dared not go to bed; he sat looking into space. The roar of London hushed till it was no more than a faint murmur, the hissing of the gas grew louder, and still Hubert sat thinking, the same thoughts battling in his brain. He looked into the future, but could see nothing but suicide. His uncle? He had applied to him before for help; there was no hope there. Then he tramped up and down, maddened by the infernal hissing of the gas; and then threw himself into his arm-chair. And so a terrible night wore away; and it was not until long after the early carts had begun to rattle in the streets that exhaustion brought an end to his sufferings, and he rolled into bed.

VI

'WHAT will ye 'ave to eat?   Eggs and bacon?'

'No, no!'

'Well, then, 'ave a chop?'

'No, no!'

'Ye must 'ave something.'

'A cup of tea, a slice of toast.   I'm not hungry.'

'Well, ye are worse than a young lady for a happetite. Miss Massey 'as sent you down these 'ere papers.'

The servant-girl laid the papers on the bed, and Hubert lay back on his pillow, so that he might collect his thoughts.   Stretching forth his hands, he selected the inevitable paper.

'For those who do not believe that our English home life is composed mainly, if not entirely, of lying, drunkenness, and conjugal infidelity, and its sequel divorce, yester evening at the Queen's Theatre must have been a sad and dismal experience.   That men and women who have vowed to love each other do sometimes prove false to their troth no reasonable

58

man will deny. With the divorce court before our
eyes, even the most enthusiastic believer in the natural
goodness and ultimate perfectibility of human nature
must admit that men and women are frail. But
drunkenness and infidelity are happily not charac-
teristic of our English homes. Then why, we ask,
should a dramatist select such a theme, and by every
artifice of dialogue force into prominence all that
is mean and painful in an unfortunate woman's life?
Always the same relentless method; the cold, passionless curiosity of the vivisector; the scalpel is placed
under the nerve, and we are called upon to watch the
quivering flesh. Never the kind word, the tears, the
effusion, which is man's highest prerogative, and which
separates him from the brute and signifies the immortal
end for which he was created. We hold that it is a
pity to see so much talent wasted, and it was indeed a
melancholy sight to see so many capable actors and
actresses labouring to——'

'This is even worse than usual,' said Hubert; and
glancing through half a column of hysterical commonplace, he came upon the following :—

'But if this woman had succeeded in reclaiming
from vice the man who unjustly divorced her, and who
in his misery goes back to ask her forgiveness for pity's

sake, what a lesson we should have had ! And, with lightened and not with heavier hearts, we should have left the theatre comforted, better and happier men and women. But turning his back on the goodness, truth, and love whither he had induced us to believe he was leading us, the author flagrantly makes the woman contradict her whole nature in the last act ; and, because her husband falls again, she, instead of raising him with all the tender mercies and humanities of wifehood, declares that her life has been one long mistake, and that she accepts the divorce which the Court had unjustly granted. The moral, if such a word may be applied to such a piece is this : " The law may be bad, but human nature is worse." '

The other morning papers took the same view,—a great deal of talent wasted on a subject that could please no one. Hubert threw the papers aside, lay back, and in the lucid idleness of the bed his thoughts grew darker. It was hardly possible that the piece could survive such notices ; and if it did not ? Well, he would have to go. But until the piece was taken out of the bills it would be a weakness to harbour the ugly thought.

There were, however, the evening papers to look forward to, and soon after midday Annie was sent to buy all that had appeared. Hubert expected to find in these papers a more delicate appreciation of his work. Many of the critics of the evening press were his personal friends, and nearly all were young men in full sympathy with the new school of dramatic thought. He read paper after paper with avidity ; and Annie was sent in a cab to buy one that had not yet found its way so far north as Fitzroy Street. The opinion of this paper was of all importance, and Hubert tore it open with trembling fingers. Although more temperately written than the others, it was clearly favourable, and Hubert sighed a sweet sigh of relief. A weight was lifted from him ; the world suddenly seemed to grow brighter ; and he went to the theatre that evening, and, half doubting and half confidently, presented himself at the door of Montague Ford's dressing-room. The actor had not yet begun to dress, and was busy writing letters. He stretched his hand hurriedly to Hubert.

'Excuse me, my dear fellow; I have a couple of letters to finish.'

Hubert sat down, glancing nervously from the actor to the morning papers with which the table was strewn. There was not an evening paper there. Had he not seen them ? At the end of about ten minutes the actor said,—

'Well, this is a bad business ; they are terribly down on us—aren't they ? What do you think ? '

'Have you seen the evening papers—*The Telephone*, for instance ? '

'Oh yes, I 've seen them all; but the evening papers don't amount to much. Stiggins's article was terrible. I am afraid he has killed the piece.'

'Don't you think it will run, then ? '

'Well, that depends upon the public, of course. If they like it, I 'll keep it on.'

'How 's the booking ? '

'Not good.' Montague Ford moved his papers absent-mindedly. At the end of a long silence he said, 'Even if the piece did catch on, it would take a lot of working up to undo the mischief of those articles. Of course you can rely on me to give it every chance. I shan't take it out of the bills if I can possibly help.'

'There is my *Gipsy*.'

'I have another piece ready to put into rehearsal; it was arranged for six months ago. I only consented to produce your play because—well, because there has been such an outcry lately about art. . . . Tremendous part for me in the new piece . . . I 'm sure you 'll like it.'

The business did improve, but so very slowly that

Hubert was afraid Ford would lose patience and take the play out of the bills. But while the fate of the play hung in the balance, Hubert's life was being rendered unbearable by duns. They had found him out, one and all; to escape being served was an impossibility; and now his table was covered with summonses to appear at the County Court. This would not matter if the piece once took the public taste. Then he would be able to pay every one, and have some time to rest and think. And there seemed every prospect of its catching on. Discussions regarding the morality of the play had arisen in the newspapers, and the eternal question whether men and women are happier married or unmarried had reached its height. Hubert spent the afternoon addressing letters to the papers, striving to fan the flame of controversy. Every evening he listened for Rose's footstep on the stairs.—How did the piece go?—Was there a better house? Money or paper?—Have you seen the notice in the——?—First-rate, wasn't it?—That ought to do some good.—I've heard there was a notice in the ——, but I haven't seen it. Have you?—No; but So-and-so saw the paper, and said there was nothing in it. And, do you know, I hear there's going to be a notice in *The Modern Review*, and that So-and-so is writing it.

Every post brought newspapers; the room was filled
with newspapers—all kinds of newspapers—papers one
has never heard of,—French papers, Welsh papers,
North of England papers, Scotch and Irish papers.
Hubert read columns about himself, anecdotes of all
kinds,—where he was born, who were his parents, and
what first induced him to attempt writing for the
stage; his personal appearance, mode of life, the cut of
his clothes; his religious, moral, and political views.
Had he been the plaintiff in an action for criminal libel,
greater industry in the collection and the fabrication of
personal details could hardly have been displayed.

But at these articles Hubert only glanced; he was
interested in his piece, not in himself, and when Annie
brought up *The Modern Review* he tore it open, knowing he would find there criticism more fundamental,
more searching. But as he read, the expression of
hope which his face wore changed to one of pain pitiful
to look upon. The article began with a sketch of the
general situation, and in a tone of commiseration, of
benevolent malice, the writer pointed out how inevitable it was that the critics should have taken Mr.
Price, when *Divorce* was first produced, for the new
dramatic genius they were waiting for. 'There comes
a moment,' said this caustic writer, 'in the affairs of

men when the new is not only eagerly accepted, but when it is confounded with the original. Wearied by the old stereotyped form of drama, the critics had been astonished by a novelty of subject, more apparent than real, and by certain surface qualities in the execution; they had hailed the work as being original both in form and in matter, whereas all that was good in the play had been borrowed from France and Scandinavia. *Divorce* was the inevitable product of the time. It had been written by Mr. Price, but it might have been written by a dozen other young men—granting intelligence, youth, leisure, a university education, and three or four years of London life—any one of à dozen clever young men who frequent West End drawing-rooms and dabble in literature might have written it. All that could be said was that the play was, or rather had been, *dans le mouvement*; and original work never is *dans le mouvement*. *Divorce* was nothing more than the product of certain surroundings, and remembering Mr. Price's other plays, there seemed to be no reason to believe that he would do better. Mr. Price had tried his hand at criticism, and that was a sure sign that the creative faculty had begun to wither. His critical essays were not rich nor abundant in thought, they were not the skirmishing of a man fighting for his ideas, they were not preliminary to a great battle ; they were at once vague and pedantic, somewhat futile, *les ébats d'un esprit en peine*, and seemed to announce a talent in progress of disintegration rather than of reconstruction.

'Sometimes the critic's phrases seemed wet with tears ; sometimes, abandoning his tone of commiseration, he would assume one of scientific indifference. The phenomenon was the commonest. There were dozens of Hubert Prices in London. The universities and the newspapers, working singly and in collaboration, turned them out by the dozen. And the mission of these men of intelligent culture seemed to be to *poser des lapins sur la jeune presse*. Each one came in turn with his little volume of poems, his little play, his little picture ; all were men of "advanced ideas " ; in other words, they were all *dans le mouvement*. There was the rough Hubert Price, who made mild consternation in the drawing-room, and there was the sophisticated Hubert Price, who cajoled the drawing-room ; there was the sincere and the insincere, and the Price that suffered and the Price that didn't. Each one brought a different *nuance*, a thousand infinitesimal variations of the type, but, considered merely in its relation to art, the species may be said to be divided

66

into two distinct categories. In the first category are those who rise almost at the first bound to a certain level, who produce quickly, never reaching again the original standard, dropping a little lower at each successive effort until their work becomes indistinguishable from the ordinary artistic commercialism of the time. The fate of those in the second category is more pathetic; they gradually wither and die away like flowers planted in a thin soil. Among these men many noble souls are to be found, men who have surrendered all things for love of their art, and who seemed at starting to be the best equipped to win, but who failed, impossible to tell how or why. Sometimes their failure turns to comedy, sometimes to tragedy. They may become refined, delicate, elderly bachelors, the ornaments of drawing-rooms, professional diners-out— men with brilliant careers behind them. But if fate has not willed that they should retire into brilliant shells; if chance does not allow them to retreat, to separate themselves from their kind, but arbitrarily joins them to others, linking their fate to the fate of others' unhappiness, disaster may and must accrue from the alliance; honesty of purpose, trueness of heart, deep love, every great, good, and gracious quality to be found in nature, will not suffice to save them.'

The paper dropped from his hands, and he re-collected all his failures.

'Once I could do good work; now I can do neither good work nor bad. Were I a rich man, I should collect my scattered papers and write songs to be sung in drawing-rooms; but being a poor one, I must—I suppose I must get out. Positively, there is no hope, —debts on every side. Fate has willed me to go as went Haydon, Gerard de Nerval, and Maréchal. The first cut his throat, the second hanged himself, and the third blew out his brains. Clearly the time has come to consider how I shall make my exit. It is a little startling to be called upon so peremptorily to go.'

In this moment of extreme dejection it seemed to Hubert that the writer of the article had told him the exact truth. He refused to admit the plea of poverty. It was of course hard to write when one is being harassed by creditors. But if he had had it in him, it would have come out. The critic had very probably told him the truth. He could not hope to make a living out of literature. He had not the strength to write the masterpiece which the perverse cruelty of nature had permitted him only to see, and he was hope-lessly unfit for journalism. But in his simple, whole-some mind there was no bent towards suicide; and he

68

scanned every horizon. Once again he thought of his uncle. Five years ago he had written, asking him for the loan of a hundred pounds. He had received ten. And how vain it would be to write a second time! A few pounds would only serve to prolong his misery. No; he would not drift from degradation to degradation.

He only glanced at the letter which Annie had brought up with the copy of *The Modern Review*. It was clearly a lawyer's letter. Should he open it? Why not spare himself the pain? He could alter nothing; and in these last days—— Leaving the thought unfinished, he sought for his keys; he went to his box, unlocked it, and took out a small paper package. Of the fifty pounds he had received from Ford about twenty remained: he had been poorer before, but hardly quite so hopeless. He scanned every horizon —all were barred. The thought of suicide, and with it the instinctive shrinking from it, came into his mind again. Suppose he took, that very night, an overdose of chloral? He tried to put the thought from him, and returned, a little dazed and helpless, to his chair. Had the critic in *The Modern Review* told him the truth? Was he incapable of earning a living? It seemed so. Above all, was he incapable of finishing

The Gipsy as he intended? No; that he felt was a
lie. Give him six months' quiet, free from worry and
all anxiety, and he would do it. Many a year had
passed since he had enjoyed a month of quiet; and
glancing again at the letter on the table, he thought
that perhaps at that very moment a score of gallery
boys were hissing his play. Perhaps at that very
moment Ford was making up his mind to announce
the last six nights of *Divorce*. At a quarter to twelve
he heard Rose's foot on the stairs. He opened the
door.

'How did the piece go to-night?'

'Pretty well.'

'Only pretty well? Won't you come in for a few
minutes? . . . So the piece didn't go very well to-
night?'

'Oh yes, it did. I've seen it go better; but——'

'Did you get a call?'

'Yes, after the second act.'

'Not after the third?'

'No. That act never goes well. Harding came
behind; I was speaking to him, and he said something which struck me as being very true. Ford, he
said, plays the part a great deal too seriously. When
the piece was first produced, it was played more good-

humouredly by indifferent actors, who let the thing
run without trying to bring out every point. Ford
makes it as hard as nails. I think those were his
exact words.'

Hubert did not answer. At the end of a long
silence he said,—

'Did you hear anything about the last night's?'

'No,' she said ; 'I heard nothing of that.'

'Ford appeared quite satisfied then?'

'Yes, quite,' she answered, with difficulty ; for his
eyes were fixed on her, and she felt he knew she was
not telling the truth. The conversation paused again,
and to turn it into another channel she said, 'Why,
you have not opened your letter!'

'I can see it is a lawyer's letter, on account of
some unpaid bill. If I could pay it, I would ; but as.
I can't——'

'You are afraid to open it,' said Rose.

Ashamed of his weakness, Hubert opened the letter,
and began to read. Rose saw that the letter was not
such an one as he had expected, and a moment after
his face told her that fortunate news had come to
him. The signs of the tumult within were represented by the passing of the hand across the brow,
as if to brush aside some strange hallucination, and

the sudden coming of a vague look of surprise and fear into the eyes. He said,—

'Read it! Read it!'

Relieved of much detail and much cumbersome legal circumlocution, it was to the following effect:— That about three months ago Mr. Burnett had come up from his place in Sussex, and at the offices of Messrs. Grandly & Co. had made a will, in which he had disinherited his adopted daughter, Miss Emily Watson, and left everything to Mr. Hubert Price. There was no question as to the validity of the will; but Messrs. Grandly deemed it their duty to inform Mr. Hubert Price of the circumstances under which it had been made, and also of the fact that a few weeks before his death Mr. Burnett had told Mr. John Grandly, who was then staying with Mr. Burnett at Ashwood, that he intended adding a codicil, leaving some two or three hundred a year to Miss Watson. It was unfortunate that Mr. Burnett had not had time to do this; for Miss Watson was an orphan, eighteen years of age, and entirely unprovided for. Messrs. Grandly begged to submit these facts to the con- sideration of Mr. Hubert Price. Miss Watson was now residing at Ashwood. She was there with a friend of hers, Mrs. Bentley; and should Mr. Hubert Price feel inclined to do what Mr. Burnett had left undone, Messrs. Grandly would have very great pleasure in carrying his wishes into effect.

'I'm not dreaming, am I?'

'No, you are not. It is quite true. Your uncle has left his money to you. I am so glad; indeed I am. You will be able to finish your play, and take a theatre and produce it yourself if you like. I hope you won't forget me. I do want to play that part. You can't quite know what I shall do with it. One can't explain oneself in a scene here and there. . . . What are you thinking of?'

'I'm thinking of that poor girl, Emily Watson. It comes very hard upon her.'

'Who is she?'

'The girl my uncle disinherited.'

'Oh, she! Well, you can marry her if you like. That would not be a bad notion. But if you do, you'll forget all about me and Lady Hayward.'

'No; I shall never forget you, Rose.' He stretched his hand to her; but, irrespective of his will, the gesture seemed full of farewell.

'I'm so much obliged to you,' he said; 'had it not been for you, I might never have opened that letter.'

'Even if you hadn't, it wouldn't have mattered; you

would have heard of your good fortune some other way. But it is getting very late. I must say good-night. I hope you will have a pleasant time in the country, and will finish your play. Good-night.'

Returning from the door, he stopped to think. 'We have been very good friends—that is all. How strangely determined she is ! . . . More so than I am. She is bound to succeed. There is in her just that note of individual passion. . . . Perhaps some one will find her out before I have finished,—that would be a pity. I wonder which of us will succeed first?'

Then the madness of good fortune came upon him suddenly; he could think no more of Rose, and had to go for a long walk in the streets.

VII

'Dearest Emily, you must prepare yourself for the worst.'

'Is he dead?'

'Yes; he passed away quite quietly. To look at him one would say he was asleep; he does not appear to have suffered at all.'

'Oh, Julia, Julia, do you think he forgave me? I could not do what he asked me. . . . I loved him very dearly as a father, but I could not have married him.'

'No, dear, you could not. Such a marriage would have been most unnatural; he was more than forty years older than you.'

'I do not think he ever thought of such a thing until about a month or six weeks ago. You remember how I ran to you? I was as white as a ghost, and I trembled like a leaf. I could hardly speak. . . . You remember?'

'Yes, I remember; and some hours after, when I came into this room, he was standing there, just there, on the hearth-rug; there was a fearful look of pain and

75

despair on his face—he looked as if he was going mad. I never saw such a look before, and I never wish to see such a look again. And the effort he made to appear unconcerned when he saw me was perhaps the worst part of it. I pretended to see nothing, and walked away towards the window and looked out. But all the while I could feel that some terrible drama was passing behind me. At last I had to look round. He was sitting in that chair, his elbows on his knees, clasping his head with both hands, the old, gnarled fingers twined in the iron-grey hair. Then, unable to contain himself any longer, he rushed out of the room, out of the house, and across the park.'

'You say that he passed away quietly; he did not seem to suffer at all?'

'No, he never recovered consciousness.'

'But do you think that my refusal to marry him had anything to do with his death?'

'Oh no, Emily; a fit of apoplexy, with a man of his age, generally ends fatally.'

'Even if I had known it all beforehand I don't think I could have acted differently. I could not have married him. Indeed I couldn't, Julia, not even if I knew I should save his life by doing so. I daresay it is very wicked of me, but——'

'Dearest Emily, you must not give way to such thoughts; you did quite right in refusing to marry Mr. Burnett. It was very wrong of him even to think of asking you, and if he had ·lived he would have seen how wrong it was of him to desire such a thing.'

'If he had lived! But then he didn't live, not even long enough to forgive me, and when we think of how much he suffered—I don't mean in dying, you say he passed away quietly, but all this last month how heart-broken he looked! You remember when he sat at the head of the table, never speaking to us, and how frightened I was lest I should meet him on the stairs; I used to stand at the door of my room, afraid to move. I know he suffered, poor old man. I was very, very sorry for him. Indeed I was, Julia, for I'm not selfish, and when I think now that he died without forgiving me, I feel, I feel—oh, I feel as if I should like to die myself. Why do such things happen to me? I feel just as miserable now as I used to when I lived with father and mother, who could not agree. I have often told you how miserable I was then, but I don't think you ever quite understood. I feel just the same now, just as if I never wanted to see any one or anything again. I was so unhappy when I was a child, they thought I would die, and I should have died if I had

remained listening to father and mother any longer.
. . . Every one thought I was so lucky when Mr.
Burnett decided to adopt me and leave me all his
money, and he has done that, poor old man, so I
suppose I should be happy; but I'm not.'

The girl's eyes turned instinctively towards the
window and rested for a moment on the fair, green
prospects of the park.

'I hated to listen to father and mother quarrelling,
but I loved them, and I had not been here a year
before father died, and darling mother was not long
following him—only six months. Then I had no one :
a few distant relatives, whom I knew nothing of, whom
I did not care for, so I gave all my love to Mr. Burnett.
He was so good to me; he never denied me anything;
he gave me everything, even you, dearest Julia. When
he thought I wanted a companion, he found you for
me. ' I learnt to love you. You became my best and
dearest friend. Then things seemed to brighten up,
and I thought I was happy, when all this dreadful
trouble came upon us. Don't let's speak of it more
than we can help. I often wished myself dead. Didn't
you, Julia?'

Emily Watson told the story of her misfortunes in a
low, musical voice, heedless of two or three interrup-

tions, hardly conscious of her listener, impressed and
interested by the fatality of circumstances which she
believed in design against her. She was a small,
slender girl of about eighteen. Her abundant chestnut
hair — exquisite, soft, and silky — was looped pic-
turesquely, and fastened with a thin tortoiseshell
comb. The tiny mouth trembled, and the large,
prominent eyes reflected a strange, yearning soul.
She was dressed in white muslin, and the fantastically
small waist was confined with a white band. Her
friend and companion, Julia Bentley, was a woman of
about thirty, well above the medium height, full-bosomed
and small-waisted. The type was Anglo-Saxon even to
commonplace. The face was long, with a look of
instinctive kindness upon it. She was given to staring,
and as she looked at Emily, her blue eyes filled with an
expression which told of a nature at once affectionate
and intelligent. She was dressed in yellow linen, and
wore a gold bracelet on a well-turned arm.

The room was a long, old-fashioned drawing-room.
It had three windows, and all three were filled with
views of the park, now growing pale in the evening
air. The flower-gardens were drawn symmetrically
about the house and were set with blue flower-vases
in which there were red geraniums. It was a very

large room, nearly forty feet long, with old portraits on the walls—ugly things and ill done; and where there were no portraits the walls were decorated with vine leaves and mountains. The parqueted floor was partially covered with skins, and the furniture seemed to have known many a generation; some of it was heavy and cumbersome, some of it was modern. There was a grand piano, and above it two full-length portraits—a lady in a blue dress and a man in black velvet knee-breeches. At the end of a long silence, Emily suddenly threw herself weeping into Julia's arms.

'Oh, you are my only friend; you will not leave me now. . . . We shall always love one another, shall we not? If anything ever came between us it would kill me. . . . That poor old man lying dead up-stairs! He loved me very dearly, and I loved him, too. Yet I said just now I could not have married him even if I had known it would save his life. I was wrong; yes, I would have married him if I had known. . . . You don't believe me?'

'My dearest girl, you must try to forget that Mr. Burnett ever entertained so foolish a thought. He was a very good man, and loved you for a long time as he should have loved you—as a daughter. We shall respect his memory best by forgetting the events of the last six weeks. And now, Emily, dinner will be ready at seven o'clock, and it is now six. What are you going to do?'

'I shall go out for a little walk. I shall go down and see the swans.'

'Shall I come with you?'

'No, thank you, dear; I think I'd sooner be alone. I want to think.'

Julia looked a moment anxiously at this fragile girl, whose tiny head was poised on a long, delicate neck like a fruit on its stem.

'Yes, go for a walk, dear,' said Julia; 'it will do you good. Shall I go and fetch your hat and jacket?'

'No, thank you, I will not trouble you; I'll go myself.'

'No, Emily, I think you had better let me go.'

'Oh, no; I am not afraid.'

And she went up the wide oak staircase, thinking of the man who lay dead in the room at the end of the passage. She was conscious of a sense of dread; the house seemed to wear a strange air, and her dog, Dandy, was conscious of it, too; he was more silent, less joyful than usual. And when she came from her room, dressed to go out, instead of rushing down-stairs, barking with joy, he dropped his tail and lingered at the end of the passage. She called him; he still hesitated, and then, yielding to a sudden desire, she went down the passage and knocked at the door of the room. The nurse answered her knock.

'Oh, don't come in, miss.'

'Why not? I want to see him before he goes away for ever.'

Upon the limp, white curtains of an old four-posted bed she saw the memorable profile—stern, unrelenting. How still he lay! Never would that face speak or laugh or see again. Although sixty-five, his head was covered with short, thick, iron-grey hair; the beard, too, was short and thick, and iron-grey. The face was rugged, and when Emily touched the coarse hand, telling of a life of toil, she started—it was singularly cold. Fear and sorrow in like measure choked her, and· her soul awoke, and tremblingly she walked out of the house, glad to breathe the sweet evening air.

She walked towards the artificial water. The sky was melancholy and grey, and the park lay before her, hushed and soundless. Through the shadows of the darkening island two swans floated softly, leaving behind slight silver lines; above, the swallows flew high in the evening. There was sensation of death,

too, in this cold, mournful water, and in the silence
that hung about it, and in some vague way it reminded
Emily of her own life. She had known little else but
death; her life seemed full of death; and those
reflections, so distinct and so colourless, were like
death.

Then, in a sudden expansion of youth she wondered.
Her own life, how strange, how personal, how intense!
What did it mean, what meaning had it in the great,
wide world? And the impressive tranquillity, the pale
death of the day, lying like a flower on the water,
seemed to symbolise her thought, and she felt more
distinctly than she had ever done before. And there
arose in her a nervous and passionate interest in
herself. She seemed so strange, so wonderful. Her
childhood was in itself an enigma. That sad and
sorrowful childhood of hers, passed in that old London
house; her mother's love for her; her cruel, stern
stepfather, and the endless quarrels between her father
and mother, which made her young life so unbearable,
so wretched, that she could never think of those years
without tears rising to her eyes. And then the going
away, coming to live with Mr. Burnett! The death of
her father and her dear mother, so sudden, following so
soon one after the other. How much there had been

in her life, how wonderful it was ! Her love of Mr.
Burnett, and then that bitter and passionate change in
him ! That proposal of marriage ; could she ever
forget it ? And then this cruel and sudden death.
Everything she had ever loved had been taken from
her. Only Julia remained, and should Julia be taken
from her, she felt that she must die. But that would
not, could not, happen. She was now mistress of
Ashwood, she was a great heiress ; and she and Julia
would live always together, they would always love one
another, they would always live here in this beautiful
place which they loved so well.

VIII

THERE were at the funeral a few personal friends who lived in the neighbourhood, the farmers on the estate, and the labourers; and when the little crowd separated outside the church, Emily and Julia walked back to Ashwood with Mr. Grandly, Mr. Burnett's intimate friend and solicitor. They returned through the park, hardly speaking at all, Emily absent-minded as usual, waving her parasol occasionally at a passing butterfly. The grass was warm and beautiful to look on, and they lingered, prolonging the walk. It was very good of Mr. Grandly to accompany them back; he might have gone on straight to the station, so Julia thought, and she was surprised indeed when, instead of bidding them good-bye at the front door, he said—

'Before I return to London I have a communication to make to both you ladies. Will it suit you to come into the drawing-room with me?'

'Perfectly, so far as I'm concerned; and you, Emily?'

'Oh, I've nothing to do; but if it is about business, Julia will attend——'

'I think you had better be present, Miss Watson.'

Mr. Grandly was a tall, massive man with benevolent features; his bald, pink skull was partly covered with one lock of white hair. There was an anxious look in his pale, deep-set eyes which impressed Julia, and she said: 'I hope this communication you have to make to us is not of a painful nature. We have——'

'Yes, Mrs. Bentley, I know that you have been severely tried lately, but there is no help for it. I cannot keep you in ignorance any longer of certain facts relating to Mr. Burnett's will.' The words 'will' and 'facts' struck on Emily's ear. She had been thinking about her fortune. The very ground she was walking on was hers. She was the owner of this beautiful park; it seemed like a fairy tale. And that house, that dear, old-fashioned house, that rambling, funny old place of all sizes and shapes, full of deep staircases and pictures, was hers. Her eyes wandered along the smooth wide drive, down to the placid water crossed by the great ornamental bridge, the island where she had watched the swans floating last night— all these things were hers. So the words 'will' and 'facts' and 'ignorance of them' jarred her clutching little dream, and she turned her eyes—they wore an anxious look—towards Mr. Grandly, and said with an authoritative air : 'Yes, let us go into the drawing-room ; I want to hear what Mr. Grandly has to say about—— Let us go into the drawing-room at once.'

Julia took the chair nearest to her. Emily stood at the window, waiting impatiently for Mr. Grandly to begin. He laid his hat on the parquet, wiped his forehead with his handkerchief, and drew an arm-chair forward. 'Mr. Burnett, as you know, made a will some years ago, in favour of his cousin and adopted daughter, Miss Emily Watson. In that will he left his entire fortune to her, Ashwood Park and all his invested money. No other person was mentioned in that will, except Miss Watson. It was I who drew up this will. I remember discussing its provisions with Mr. Burnett, and advising him to leave something, even if it were only a few hundred pounds, to his nephew, Hubert Price. But Mr. Burnett was always a very headstrong man ; he had quarrelled with this young man, as he said, irreparably, and could not be induced to leave him even a hundred pounds. I thought this was harsh, and as Mr. Burnett's friend I told him so—I have always been opposed to extreme measures,—but he was not to be gainsaid. So the matter remained for many years; never did Mr. Burnett mention his nephew's name. I thought he had forgotten the young man's existence, when, suddenly, without warning, Mr. Burnett came into my office and told me that he intended to alter his will, leaving all his property to his nephew, Hubert Price. You know what old friends we were, and, presuming on our friendship, I told him what I thought of his project of disinheritance, for it amounted to that. Well, suffice it to say, we very nearly quarrelled over the matter. I refused to draw up the will, so iniquitous did it seem to me. He said : "Very well, Grandly, I'll go elsewhere." Then I remembered that if I allowed him to go elsewhere I should lose all hold over him, and I consented to draw up the will.'

Emily listened, a vague expression of pain in her pathetic eyes. Then this house, this room where she was sitting, was not hers, and a strange man would come soon and drive her away !

'And he has left Ashwood to Mr. Price, is not that his name?' she said, abruptly.

'Yes; he has left Ashwood to Mr. Price.'

'And when did he make this new will?'

'I think it is just about a month ago.'

Emily leaned forward, and her great eyes, full of light and sorrow, were fixed in space, her little pale hands linked, and the great mass of chestnut hair slipping from the comb. She was, in truth, at that moment the subject of a striking picture, and she was even more impressive when she said, speaking slowly : 'Then that old man was even wickeder than I thought. Oh, what I have learned in the last three or four weeks ! Oh, what wickedness, what wickedness ! . . . But go on,' she said, looking at Mr. Grandly ; 'tell me all.'

'I suppose there was some very serious reason, but on that point Mr. Burnett absolutely refused to answer me. He said his reasons were his own, and that he intended to leave his money to whom he pleased.'

'There was——' Julia stopped short, and looked interrogatively at Emily.

'Go on, Julia, tell him ; we have nothing to conceal.'

'Mr. Burnett asked Emily to marry him a short time ago ; she, of course, refused, and ever since he seemed more like——'

'A madman than anything else,' broke in Emily. 'Oh, for the last month we have led a miserable life ! It was a happy release.'

'Is it possible,' said Mr. Grandly, 'that Mr. Burnett seriously contemplated marriage with Miss Watson ?'

'Yes, and her refusal seemed to drive him out of his mind.'

'I never was more surprised.' The placid face of the eminently respectable solicitor lapsed into contemplation. 'I often tried,' he said, suddenly, 'to divine the reason why he changed his will. Disappointed love seemed the only conceivable reason, but I rejected it as being quite inconceivable. Well, it only shows how little we know what is passing in each other's minds.'

'Then,' said Julia, 'Mr. Burnett has divided his fortune, leaving Ashwood to Mr. Price, and all his invested money to Emily?'

A look of pain passed over Mr. Grandly's benevolent face, and he answered : 'Unfortunately he has left everything to Mr. Price.'

'I'm glad,' exclaimed Emily, 'that he has left me nothing. Once he thought fit to disinherit me because I would not marry him, I prefer not to have anything to do with his money.'

Mr, Grandly and Julia looked at each other; they did not need to speak ; each knew that the girl did not realise at once the full and irretrievable nature of this misfortune. The word 'destitute' was at present unrealised, and she only thought that she had been deprived of what she loved best in the world—Ashwood. Mr. Grandly glanced at her, and then speaking a little more hurriedly, said—

'I was saying just now that I only consented to draw up the will so that I might be able at some future time to induce Mr. Burnett to add a codicil to it. Later on I spoke to him again on the subject, and he promised to consider it, and a few days after he wrote to me, saying that he had decided to take my advice and add a codicil. Subsequently, in another letter he mentioned three hundred a year as being the sum he thought he would be in honour bound to leave Miss Watson. Unfortunately, he did not live long enough to carry this intention into execution. But the letters he addressed to me on the subject exist, and I have every hope that the heir, Mr. Price, will be glad to make some provision for his cousin.'

'Have you any reason for thinking that Mr. Price will do so?' said Julia.

'No. But it seems impossible for any honourable man to act otherwise.'

'He cannot bear enmity against Emily, who of course knew nothing of his quarrel with his uncle. Do you know anything about Mr. Price? What is he? Where does he live?'

'He is a literary man, I believe. I have heard that he writes plays!'

'Oh, a writer of plays.'

'Yes. I am glad of it; he may be easier to deal with. I daresay it is a mistaken notion, but one is apt to imagine that these artist folk are more generous with their money than ordinary mortals.'

'Is he married?' said Julia, and involuntarily she glanced toward Emily.

Mr. Grandly, too, looked toward the girl, and then he said: 'I don't know if Mr. Price is married; I hope not.'

'Why do you hope so?' said Emily, suddenly.

'Because if he isn't, there will only be one person to deal with. If he had a wife, she would have a voice in the matter; and in such circumstances as ours a man is easier to deal with. I earnestly hope Mr. Hubert Price is not married, and shall consider it a great point in our favour if on returning to town I find he is not.' Then assuming a lighter tone, for the nervous strain of the last ten minutes had been intense, he said: 'If he is not married, who knows—you may take a fancy to him, and he to you; then things would be just the same as before—only better.'

'I should not marry him—I hate him already. I wonder how you can think of such a thing, Mr. Grandly? You know that he must be a very wicked man for uncle to have disinherited him. I have always heard that

—but I don't know what I am saying.' Tears welled up into her eyes. 'I daresay my cousin is not so bad as—but I can talk no more. . . . I am very miserable, I have always been miserable, and I don't know why; I never did harm to any one.'

Soon after Mr. Grandly bade the ladies good-bye. Julia followed him to the front door. 'You will do all you can to help us? That poor child is too young, too inexperienced, to realise what her position is.'

'I know, I know,' said Mr. Grandly, extending both hands to Julia; 'in the whole course of my experience I never met with a sadder case. But we must not take too sad a view of it. Perhaps all will come right in the end. The young man cannot refuse to make good his uncle's intentions. He cannot see his cousin go to the workhouse. I will do the best I can for you. The moment I get back to London, I'll set inquiries on foot and find out his address, and when I have seen him I'll write. Good-bye.'

Then, resolving that it were better to leave the girl to herself, Julia took up her key-basket and hurried away on household business. But in the middle of her many occupations she would now and then stop short to think. She had never heard of anything so cruel before. That poor girl—she must go to her; she must

not leave her alone any longer. But it would be well
to avoid the subject as much as possible. She must
think of something to distract her thoughts. The pony-
chaise. It might be the last time they had a carriage
to go out in. But they could not go out driving on the
day of the funeral.

That evening, as they were going to bed, Emily said,
lifting her sweet, pathetic little face, looking all love
and gentleness: 'Oh, to think of a common, vulgar
writer coming here, with a common, vulgar wife and a
horrid crowd of children. Oh, Julia, doesn't it seem
impossible? And yet I suppose it is true. I cannot
bear to think of it. I can see the horrid children
tramping up and down the stairs, breaking the things
we have known and loved so long; and they will
destroy all my flowers, and no one will remember to
feed the poor swans. Dandy, my beloved, I shall be
able to take you with me.' And she caught up the
rough-haired terrier and hugged him, kissing his
dear old head. 'Dandy is mine; they can't take him
from me, can they? But do you think the swans
belong to them or to us? I suppose it would be
impossible to take them with us if we go to live in
London. They couldn't live in a backyard.'

'But, dearest Emily, who are "they"? You don't

know that he is married—literary men don't often marry. For all you know, he is a handsome young man, who will fall madly in love with you.'

'No one ever fell in love with me except that horrid old man—how I hate him, how I detest to think of it! I thought I should have died when he asked to marry me. The very memory of it is enough to make me hate all men, and prevent me from liking any one. I don't think I could like him; I should always see that wicked old man's hoary, wrinkled face in his.'

'Oh, Emily, I cannot think how such ideas can come into your head. It is not right, indeed it isn't.' And this simple Englishwoman looked at this sensitive girl in sheer wonderment and alarm.

'I only say what I think. I am glad the old man did disinherit me. I'm glad we are leaving Ashwood; I cannot abide the place when I think of him. . . . There, that is his chair. I can see him sitting in it now. He is grinning at us; he is saying, "Ha! ha! I have made beggars of you both." You remember how we used to tremble when we met his terrible old face on the stairs; you remember how he used to sit glaring at us all through dinner?'

'Yes, Emily, I remember all that; but I do not think it natural that you should forget all the years of kindness ; he was very good to you, and loved you very much, and if he forgot himself at the end of his life, we must remember the weakness of age.'

'The hideousness of age,' Emily replied, in a low tone. The conversation paused, and then Julia said—

'You are speaking wildly, Emily, and will live to regret your words. Let us speak no more of Mr. Burnett. . . . I daresay you will find your cousin a charming young man. I should laugh if it were all to end in a marriage. And how glad I should be to see you off on your honeymoon, to bid you good-bye !'

'Oh, Julia, don't speak like that; you will never bid me good-bye. You will never leave me—promise me that—you are my only friend. Oh, Julia, promise me that you will never leave me.'

Tears rose in Julia's eyes, and taking the girl in her arms, she said, ' I 'll never leave you, my dear girl, until you yourself wish it.'

'I wish it ? Oh, Julia, you do not know me. I have lost everything, Julia, but I mustn't lose you. . . . After all, it doesn't so much matter, so long as we are not separated. I don't care about money, and we can have a nice little house in London all to ourselves. And if we get too hard up, we 'll both go out as daily governesses. I think I could teach a little music, to

young children, you know ; you 'd teach the older ones.'
Emily looked at Julia inquiringly, and going over to the
piano, attempted to play her favourite polka.   Julia,
who had once worked for her daily bread, and earned
it in a sort of way by giving music-lessons, smiled sadly
at the girl's ignorance of life.

'I see,' said Emily, who was quick to divine every
shade of sentiment passing in the minds of those she
loved ; 'you don't think I could teach even the little
children.'

'My dear Emily, I hope it will never come to your
having to try.'

'I must do something to get a living,' she replied,
looking vaguely and wistfully into the fire.   'How
unfortunate all this is—that horrid, horrid old man.
But supposing he had asked you to marry him—he
wasn't nice, but you are older than I, and if you
had married him you would have become, in a way,
my stepmother.   But what a charming stepmother !   Oh,
how I should have loved that !'

'Come, Emily, it is time to go to bed ; you let your
imagination run away with you.'

'Julia, you are not cross because——'

'No, dear, I 'm not cross.   I 'm only a little tired.
We have talked too long.'

Emily's allusion to music-teaching had revived in Julia all her most painful memories. If this man were to cast them penniless out of Ashwood! Supposing, supposing that were to happen? Starving days, pale and haggard, rose up in her memory. What should she do, what should she do, and with that motherless girl dependent on her for food and clothes and shelter? She buried her face in the pillow and prayed that she might be saved from such a destiny.

If this man—this unknown creature—were to refuse to help them, she and Emily would have to go to London, and she would have to support Emily as best she might. She would hold to her and fight for her with all her strength, but would she not fall vanquished in the fight ; and then, and then ? The same thoughts, questions, and fears turned in her head like a wheel, and it was not until dawn had begun to whiten the window-panes that she fell asleep.

A few days after, the post brought a letter for Julia. After glancing hastily down the page she said : 'This is a letter from Mr. Grandly, and it is good news. Oh, what a relief! . . .'

'Read it.'

'"DEAR MRS. BENTLEY,—Immediately I arrived in London, I set to work to find out Mr. Price's address. It

was the easiest matter in the world, for he has a play now
running at one of the theatres. So I directed my letter to
the theatre, and next morning I had a visit from him.
After explaining to him the resources of the brilliant
fortune he had come into, I told him of his uncle's intention
to add a codicil to his will, leaving Miss Watson three
hundred a year ; I told him that this last will had left her
entirely unprovided for. He said, at once, that he fully
agreed with me, and that he would consider what was
the most honourable course for him to take in regard to his
cousin. This is exactly what he said, but his manner was
such that before leaving he left no doubt in my mind whatever that he will act very generously indeed. I should not
be surprised if he settled even more than the proposed
three hundred a year on Miss Watson. He is a very quiet,
thoughtful young man of about two or three and thirty.
He looks poor, and I fancy he has lived through very hard
times. He wears an air of sadness and disappointment
which makes him attractive, and his manners are gentle and
refined. I tell you these things, for I know they will interest you. I have not been able to find out if he is married,
but I am sorry to say that his play has not succeeded. I
should have found out more, but he was not in my office
above ten minutes ; he had to hurry away to keep an
appointment at the theatre, for, as he explained, it was to
be decided that very day if the play was to be taken out of
the bills at the end of the week. He promised to call again,
and our interview is fixed for eleven o'clock the day after
to-morrow. In the meantime take heart, for I think I
am justified in telling you I feel quite sanguine as to the
result." '

'Well,' said Julia, laying down the letter, 'I don't think that anything could be more satisfactory, and just fancy dear old Mr. Grandly being able to describe a young man as well as that.'

'He doesn't say if he is short or tall, or dark or fair.'

'No, he doesn't. I think he might have told us something about his personal appearance, but it is a great relief to hear that he is not the vulgar Bohemian we have always understood him to be. Mr. Grandly says his manners are refined ; you might take a fancy to him after all.'

'But you don't know that he isn't married. I suppose Mr. Grandly wasn't able to find that out. I should like to know—but not because I want to marry him or any one else; only I don't like the idea of a great, vulgar woman, and a pack of children scampering about.the place when we go.'

'Do you dislike children so much, then, Emily?'

'I don't know that I ever thought about them; but I'm sure I shouldn't like his children. I dreamt of him last night. Do you believe in dreams?'

'What did you dream?'

'I cannot remember, but I woke up crying, feeling more unhappy than I ever felt in my life before. It is curious that I should dream of him last night, and that you should receive that letter this morning, isn't it?'

'I don't see anything strange in it. Nothing more natural than that you should dream about him, and it was certain that I should receive a letter from Mr. Grandly; he promised to write to me in a few days.'

'Then you believe what is in that letter—I don't. Something tells me that he will not act kindly, but I don't know how.'

'I'm quite sure you are wrong, Emily. Mr. Grandly would never have written this letter unless he knew for certain that Mr. Price would do all or more than he promised.'

'I can't see from the letter that he has promised anything. . . . Even if he does give me three hundred a year, I shall have to leave Ashwood.'

'My dear Emily, I'm cross with you: of course, if you will insist on always looking at the melancholy side. . . . Now I'm going; I've to see after the housekeeping. Are you going into the garden?'

'Yes, presently.'

Emily did not seem to know what she was going to do. She looked out of the window, she lingered in the corridor; finally she wandered into the library. The quaint, old-fashioned room recalled her childhood to her. It was here she used to learn her lessons. Here was the mahogany table, at which she used to sit with her governess, learning to read and write; and there, far away at the other end of the long room, was the round table, where lay the old illustrated editions of *Gulliver's Travels* and *The Arabian Nights*, which she used to run to whenever her governess left the room. And at the bottom of the book-cases there were drawers full of strange papers; these drawers she used to open in fear and trembling, so mysterious did they seem to her. And there was the book-cases full of the tall folios, behind which lay, in dark and dim recesses, stores of books which she used to pull out, expecting at every moment to come upon long-forgotten treasures. She smiled now, as she recalled these childish imaginings, and lifting tenderly the coarse drugget, she looked at the great green globe which her fingers used to turn in infantile curiosity.

Then leaving the library, she roamed through the house, pausing on the first landing to gaze on the picture of the fine gentleman in a red coat, his hand for ever on his sword. She remembered how she used to wonder whom he was going to kill, and how sure she used to feel that at last he would grant his adver-

sary his life. And close by was the picture of the
wind-mill, set on the edge of the down, with the
shepherd driving sheep in the foreground. Her
whole life seemed drenched with tears at the thought
of parting with these things. Every room was full of
memories for her. She was a little girl when she came
to live at Ashwood, and the room at the top of the
stairs had been her nursery. There were the two beds;
both were now dismantled and bare. It was in the
little bed in the corner that she used to sleep; it was
in the old four-poster that her nurse slept. And there
was the very place, in front of the fire, where she used
to have her tea. The table had disappeared, and the
grate, how rusty it was! In the far corner, by the
window, there used to be a press, in which nurse kept
tea and sugar. That press had been removed. The
other press was there still, and throwing open the doors
she surveyed the shelves. She remembered the very
peg on which her hat and jacket used to hang. And
the long walks in the great park, which was to her, then,
a world of wonderment!

She wandered about the old corridor, in and out of
odd rooms, all associated with her childhood—quaint
old rooms, many of them lumber rooms, full of odd
corners and old cupboards, the meaning of which she

used to strive to divine. How their silence and mystery used to thrill her little soul! Faded rooms whose mystery had departed, but whose gloom was haunted with tenderest recollections. In one corner was the reading-chair in which Mr. Burnett used to sit. At that time she used to sit on his knee, and when the chair gave way beneath their weight, he had said she was too big a girl to sit on his knee any longer. The words had seemed to her a little cruel. She had forgotten the old chair, but now she remembered the very moment when the servants came to take it away.

Under the window were some fragments of a china bowl which she had broken when quite a little child. There was a hoop-stick and the hoop which had been taken down to the blacksmith's to be mended. He had mended it, but she did not remember ever using it again. And there was an old box of water-colours, with which she used to colour all the uncoloured drawings in her picture-books. Emily took the hoop-stick, the old doll, and the broken box of water-colours, and packed them away carefully. She would be able to find room for them in the little house in London where she and Julia were going to live.

A few days after, the post brought letters from Mr.

Grandly, one for Emily and one for Julia.   Julia's
letter ran as follows :

'DEAR MRS. BENTLEY,—I write by this post to Miss
Watson, advising her that her cousin, Mr. Price, is most
anxious to make her acquaintance, and asking her to send
the dog-cart to-morrow to meet him at the station.   I must
take upon myself the responsibility for this step.   I have
seen Mr. Price again, and he has confirmed me in my
good opinion of him.   He seems most anxious, not only to
do everything right, but to make matters as pleasant
and agreeable as possible for his cousin.   He has written
me a letter recognising Miss Watson's claim upon him,
and constituting himself her trustee.   I have not had yet
time to prepare a deed of gift, but there can be little doubt
that Miss Watson's position is now quite secure.   So far
so good ; but more than ever does the only clear and
satisfactory way out of this miserable business seem to
me to be a marriage between Mr. Hubert Price and Miss
Watson.   I have already told you that he is a nice, refined
young man, of gentlemanly bearing, good presence, and
excellent speech, though a trifle shy and reserved ; and, as
I have since discovered that he is not married, I have
taken upon myself the responsibility of advising him to
jump into a train and to go and tell his cousin the conclusion he has come to regarding the will of the late Mr.
Burnett.   As I have said, he is a shy man, and it was some
time before I could induce him to take so decisive a step ;
he wanted to meet Miss Watson in my office, but I succeeded in persuading him.   He will go down to you to-
morrow by the five o'clock, and I need not impress upon

105

you the necessity that you should use your influence with Miss Watson, and that his reception should be as cordial as circumstances permit. I have only to add that I see no need that you should show this letter to Miss Watson, for the very fact of knowing that we desired to bring about a marriage might prejudice her against this young man, whom she otherwise cannot fail to find charming.'

Hearing some one at her door, Julia put the letter away. It was Emily.

'I've just received a letter from Mr. Grandly, saying that that man is coming here to-day, and that we are to send the dog-cart for him.'

'Is not that the very best thing that——'

'We cannot remain here, we must leave a note for him, or something of that kind. I wouldn't remain here to meet him for worlds. I really couldn't, Julia.'

'And why not, Emily?'

'To meet the man who is coming to turn me out of Ashwood!'

'How do you know that he is coming to turn you out of Ashwood? You imagine these things. . . . Do you suppose that Mr. Grandly would send him down here if he did not know what his intentions were?'

'But we shall have to leave Ashwood.'

'Very likely, but not in the way you imagine. Remember, Mr. Price is your cousin; you may like him very much. Let's be guided by Mr. Grandly; I have not seen your letter, but apparently he advises us to remain here and receive him.'

'I don't think I can, Julia. I have misgivings.'

'Have you been dreaming again?'

'No; I've not been dreaming, but I have misgivings.'

'You are a silly little goose, Emily. Come and give me a kiss, and promise to take my advice.'

'Dearest Julia, you do love me, don't you? Promise me that we shall not be separated, and then I don't mind.'

'Yes, dear, I promise you that, and you will promise me to try to like your cousin?'

'I'll try, Julia, but I'm awfully frightened, and—I don't think I could like him, no matter what he was like. I feel a sort of hatred in my heart. Don't you know what I mean?' And the girl looked questioningly into her friend's eyes.

'I AM Miss Watson,' she said in her low musical voice, 'and this is my friend, Mrs. Bentley.' Hubert bowed, and sought for words. He found none, and the irritating silence was broken again by Miss Watson. 'Won't you sit down?' she said.

'Thank you.' He pulled off his gloves. The pained, troubled look which he had met in Miss Watson's face seemed a reproach, and he regretted not having followed his own idea, and invited the young lady to meet him at Mr. Grandly's office. He glanced nervously from one lady to the other.

'I hope you have had a pleasant journey, Mr. Price,' said Mrs. Bentley. 'The country is looking very beautiful just at present. Do you know this part of the country?' Mrs. Bentley's words were very welcome, and Hubert replied eagerly—

'No; I do not know the country at all well. I have been very little out of London for some years, but I hope now to see more of the country. This is a beautiful place.'

At that moment he met Mrs. Bentley's eyes, and, feeling that he was touching on delicate ground, he stopped speaking. When he turned his head, he met Miss Watson's-great sad eyes, which seemed to absorb the entire face, fixed upon him. They expressed such depth of pathetic appeal that he trembled with apprehension, and the instinct in him was to beg for pardon. But it became suddenly necessary to say something, and, speaking at random, his head full of whirling words, he said—

'Of course nothing could be more sad than my poor uncle's death,—so unexpected. . . . Having lived so long together, you must have——' Then it was Hubert's turn to look appealingly at Miss Watson; but her great eyes seemed to say, 'Go on, go on; heap cruelty on cruelty!' Then he plunged desperately, hoping to retrieve his mistakes. 'He died about a month ago. Mr. Grandly told me I should still find you here, so I thought——'

The intensity of his emotion perhaps caused Hubert to accentuate his words, so that they conveyed a meaning different from that which he intended. Certainly his hesitations were capable of misinterpretation, and Miss Watson said, her voice trembling,—

'Of course we know we have no right here, we are

intruding; but we are making preparations. . . . I daresay that to-morrow we shall be able to——'

'Oh, I beg pardon, Miss Watson; let me assure you . . . I am sorry if——'

Taking a little handkerchief out of her black dress, Emily covered her face in her thin, tiny hands. She sobbed aloud, and ran out of the room. Hubert turned to Mrs. Bentley, his face full of consternation.

'I am very sorry, but she did not give me time to speak. Will you go and fetch her, Mrs. Bentley? I want to tell her I hope she will never leave Ashwood. . . I believe she thinks that I came down here to ask her to leave as soon as possible. It is really quite awful that she should think such a thing.'

'She is an exceedingly sensitive girl, and is now a little overwrought. The events of the last month have proved too much for her.'

'Mr. Grandly informed me that it was Mr. Burnett's intention to add a codicil to his will, leaving Miss Watson three hundred a year. This money I am prepared to give her, and I'm quite sure she is welcome to stay here as long as she pleases. Indeed, she will do me a great favour by remaining. Please go and tell her. I cannot bear to see a girl cry; to hear her sob like that is quite terrible.'

'You will be able to tell her yourself during the course of the evening. I think it will come better from you.'

'After what has happened, it will be very difficult for me to meet her until she is informed that she is mistaken. I charged Mr. Grandly to explain everything in his letter. Apparently he omitted to do so.'

'He only said you wanted to see Emily on a matter of business. Of course we did not expect such generosity.'

They were standing quite close together, and suddenly Hubert became conscious of Mrs. Bentley's beauty. Her blue eyes were at that moment full of tender admiration for the instinctive generosity which Hubert so unwittingly exhibited, and her eyes told what was passing in her soul. Suddenly they both seemed to understand each other better, and, playing with the bracelet on her arm, she said—

'You do not know Emily; she is strangely sensitive. But I will go and try to persuade her to return. . . . Although only distantly related, you are cousins, after all—are you not?'

'Yes, we are cousins, but the relationship is remote. Tell her everything; beg of her to come down-stairs.'

Hubert imagined Emily's little black figure thrown

upon her bed, sobbing convulsively. He was very
much agitated, and looked about the room, at first
hardly seeing it. At last its novelty drew his thoughts
from his cousin's tears, and he wondered what was the
history of the house. 'The old man,' he thought,
'bought it all, furniture and ancestors, from some
ruined landowner, and attempted very few alterations
—that's clear.' Then he reproached himself. ' How
could I have been so stupid? I did not know what I
was saying. I was so horribly nervous. Those strange
eyes of hers quite upset me. I do hope Mrs. Bentley
will tell her that I wish to act generously, that I am
prepared to do everything in my power to make her
happy. Poor little thing! She looks as if she had
never been happy.' Again the room drew Hubert's
thoughts away from his cousin. It was still lit with
the faint perfumed glow of the sunset. The paint of
the old decorations was cracked and faded. A man
in a plum-coloured coat with gold facings fixed his
eyes upon him, and the tall lady in blue satin had no
doubt played there in short clothes. He walked up
and down, he turned over the music on the piano, and,
hearing a step, looked round. It was only the servant
coming to tell him that his room was ready.

He dressed for dinner, hoping to find the two ladies

in the drawing-room, and it was a disappointment to find only Mrs. Bentley there.

'I have told Emily everything you said. She is very grateful, and begs of me to thank you for your kind intentions. But I am afraid you must excuse her absence from dinner. I really don't think she is in a fit state to come down; she couldn't possibly take part in the conversation.'

'But why? I hope she isn't ill? Had we better send for the doctor?'

'Oh no; she'll be all right in the morning. She has been crying. She suffers from depression of spirits. She is, I assure you, all right,' said Mrs. Bentley, replying to Hubert's alarmed and questioning face. 'I assure you there is no need for you to reproach yourself. Dinner is ready.' She took his arm, and they went into the dining-room.

No further mention was made of Mr. Burnett, of money matters, or of the young lady up-stairs; and with considerable tact Mrs. Bentley introduced the subject of literature, alluding gracefully to Hubert's position as a dramatist.

'Your play, *Divorce*, is now running at the Queen's Theatre?'

No; I'm sorry to say it was taken out of the bills

last Saturday. Saturday night was the last performance.'

'That was not a long run. And the papers spoke
so favourably of it.'

'It is a play that only appeals to the few.' And,
encouraged by Mrs. Bentley's manner, Hubert told
her how happy endings and comic love-scenes were
essential to secure a popular success.

'I am afraid you will think me very stupid, but I
do not quite understand.'

In a quiet, unobtrusive way Hubert was a graceful
talker, and he knew how to adapt his theme, and bring
it within the circle of the sympathies of his listeners.
There was some similarity of temperament between
himself and Mrs. Bentley ; they were both quiet, fair,
meditative Saxons. She lent her whole mind to the
conversation, interested in the account that the young
man gave of his dramatic aspirations.

From the dining-room window looking over the
park the long road wound through the vaporous
country. The town stood in the middle distance, its
colour blotted out, and its smoke hardly distinguish-
able. In the room a yellow dress turned grey, and
the gold of a bracelet grew darker, and the pink of
delicate finger-nails was no longer visible. But the

pensive dusk of the dining-room, which blackened the claret in the decanters, leaving only the faintest ruby glow in the glass which Hubert raised to his lips, suited the tenor of the conversation, which had wandered from the dramatic to the social side of the question. What did he think of divorce? She sighed, and he wondered what her story might be.

They passed out of the dining-room, and stood on the gravel, watching the night gathering in the open country. In the light of the moon, which had just risen above the woods, the white road grew whiter, the town was faintly seen in the tide of blue vapour, which here and there allowed a field to appear. In the foreground a great silver fir, spiky and solitary, rose up in the blue night. Beyond it was seen a corner of the ornamental bridge. The island and its shadow were one black mass rising from the park up to the level of the moon, which, a little to the right, between the town and the island, lay reflected in a narrow strip of water. Farther away some reeds were visible in the illusive light, and the meditative chatter of dozing ducks stirred the silence which wrapped the country like a cloak.

Hubert and Mrs. Bentley stood looking at the landscape. The fragrance of his cigar, the presence of the woman, the tenderness of the hour, combined to make him strangely happy; his past life seemed to him like a harsh, cruel pain that had suddenly ceased. More than he had ever desired seemed to be fulfilled; the reality exceeded the dream. What greater happiness than to live here, and with this woman! His thoughts paused, for he had forgotten the girl up-stairs. She was not happy; but he would make her happy—of that he was quite certain. At that moment Mrs. Bentley said—

'I hope you like your home. Is not the prospect a lovely one?'

'Yes; but I was thinking at that moment of Emily. I suppose I must accustom myself to call her by her Christian name. She is my cousin, and we are going to live together. But, by the way, she cannot stay here alone. I hope—I may trust that you will remain with her?'

Mrs. Bentley turned her face towards him; he noticed the look of pleasure that had passed into it.

'Thank you; it is very good of you. I shall be glad to remain with Emily as long as she cares for my society. It is needless to say I shall do my best to deserve your approval.'

"THEY DINED AT THE CAFÉ ROYAL."

Her voice fell, and he heard her sigh, and in his happiness it seemed to him to be a pity that he should find unhappiness in others.

They went into the drawing-room. Mrs. Bentley asked him if he liked music, and she went to the piano and sang some Scotch songs very sweetly. Then she took a book from the table and bade him good-night. She was sure that he would excuse her. She must go and see after Emily.

When the door closed, the woman who had just left him seemed like some one he had seen in a dream; and still more shadowy and illusive did the girl seem—that pale and plaintive beauty, looking like a pastel, who had so troubled him with her enigmatic eyes! And the lodging-house that he had left only a few hours ago! and Rose.

On Sunday he had taken Rose out to dinner. They dined at the Café-Royal. He had tried to talk to her about Hamilton Brown's new drama, which they had just heard would follow *Divorce*; but he was unable to detach his thoughts from Ashwood and the ladies he was going to visit to-morrow evening. Hubert and Rose had felt like two school-fellows, one of whom is leaving school; the link that had bound them had snapped; henceforth their ways lay separate; and they were sad at parting just as school-friends are sad.

'You are not rich; you offered to lend me money once. I want to lend you some now.'

'Oh yes; five shillings, wasn't it?'

'It doesn't matter what the sum was—we were both very poor then——'

'And I'm still poorer now.'

'All the more reason why you should allow me to help you. . . . Allow me to write you a cheque for a hundred pounds. I assure you I can afford it.'

'I think I had better not. . . . I have some things I can sell.'

'But you must not sell your things. Indeed, you must allow me——'

'I think I'd rather not. I shall be all right—that is to say, if Ford engages me for Brown's new piece; and I think he will.'

'But if he doesn't?'

'Then,' she said, with a sweet and natural smile, 'I'll write to you. . . . We have been excellent friends—comrades—have we not?'

'Yes, we have indeed, and I shall never forget. There is my address; that will always find me.'

He had written a play—a play that the most com-

petent critics had considered a work of genius; in any
case, a play that had interested his generation more
than any other. It had failed, and failed twice; but
did that prove anything? Fortune had deserted him,
and he had been unable to finish *The Gipsy*. Was it
the fault of circumstances that he had not been able
to finish that play? or was it that the slight vein of
genius that had been in him once had been exhausted?
He remembered the article in *The Modern Review*, and
was frightened to think that the critic might have
divined the truth. Once it had seemed impossible to
finish that play; but fortune had come to his aid,
accident had made him master of his destiny; he could
spend three years, five years if he liked, on *The Gipsy*.
But why think of the play at all? What did it matter
even if he never wrote it? There were many things
to do in life besides writing plays. There was life!
His life was henceforth his own, and he could live it
as he pleased. What should he do with it? To
whom should he give it? Should he keep it all
for himself and his art? It were useless to make
plans. All he knew for certain was that henceforth
he was master of his own life, and could dispense
it as he pleased.

And then, in sensuous curiosity, his thoughts turned

on the pleasure of life in this beautiful house, in the society of two charming women.

'Perhaps I shall marry one of them. Which do I like the better? I haven't the least idea.' And then, as his thoughts detached themselves, he remembered Emily's tears.

X

It was a day of English summer, and the meadows and trees drowsed in the moist atmosphere; a few white clouds hung lazily in the blue sky; the garden was bright with geraniums and early roses, and the closely cropped privets were in full leaf. Hubert's senses were taken with the beauty of the morning, and there came the thought, so delicious, 'All this is mine.' He noticed the glitter of the greenhouses, and thought the cawing of some young rooks a sweet sound; a great tortoiseshell cat lay basking in the middle of the greensward, whisking its furry tail. Hubert stroked the animal; it arched its back, and rubbed itself against his legs. At that moment a half-bred fox-terrier barked noisily at him; he heard some one calling the dog, and saw a slight black figure hastening down one of the side-walks. Despite the dog's attempts on his legs, he ran forward.

'Emily! Emily!' he called. She stopped, turned, and stood looking at him.

'My dear cousin,' he said. 'I'm sorry about last night. I hope that Mrs. Bentley' has told you. I begged of her to do so.'

'Yes; she told me of your kind intentions. I have to thank you.'

They walked on in silence, neither knowing what to say.

'Go away, Dandy!' said Emily, thrusting her black silk parasol at the dog, who had begun an attack on Hubert's trousers. The dog retreated; Hubert laughed.

'I'm afraid he doesn't like me.'

'He'll soon get to know you. Are you fond of animals?'

'I don't know that I am, particularly.'

'Oh!' she said, looking at him reproachfully, 'how can you?' Her eyes seemed to say, 'I never can like you after that.' 'I adore animals,' she said. 'My dear dog—there is nothing in the world I love as I love my Dandy; come here, dear.' The dog came, wagging his tail, putting back his ears, knowing he was going to be caressed. Emily stooped down, took his rough head in her hands, and kissed him. 'Is he not a dear?' she said, looking up; and then she said, 'I hope you won't object to having him in the house;' her face clouded.

'Oh, my dear Emily, how can you ask such a question? I shall never object to anything you desire.' The conversation paused, and they walked some paces in silence. Emily had just begun to speak of her flowers, when they came upon the gardener, who was standing in consternation over the fragments of a broken mowing-machine. Jack—that was the donkey —had been left to himself just for a moment. It was impossible to say what wild freak had taken him; but instead of waiting, as he was expected to wait, stolidly, he had started off on a wild career, regardless of the safety of the machine. At the first bound it had come in contact with a flower-vase, which had been sent in many pieces over the sward; at the second it had met with some stone coping; and at the third it had turned over in complete dissolution, and Jack was free to tear up the turf with his hoofs, until finally his erratic course was stopped by the small boy who was responsible for the animal's behaviour. The arrival of Hubert and Emily saved the small boy from many a cuff and the donkey from a kick or two; and Jack stood amid the ruin he had created, as quiet and as docile a creature as the mind could imagine.

'Oh, you—you wicked Jack! Who would have

thought it of you ?' said Emily, throwing her arms round the animal's neck. 'And at your age, too! This is my old donkey,' she said, turning her dreamy eyes on Hubert. 'I used to ride him every day until about two years ago. I love my dear old Jack, and would not have him beaten for worlds, although he is so wicked as to break the mowing-machine. Look what you have done to the flower-vase.' The animal shook its long ears.

Hubert and Emily strolled down a long walk, wondering what they should talk about.

'These are really very pretty grounds,' he said at last. 'I am sure I shall enjoy myself immensely here.' The remark appeared to him to be of doubtful taste, and he hastened to add, 'That is to say, if I have completely made it up with my pretty cousin.'

'But you have not seen the place yet,' she said, speaking still with a certain tremor in her voice. 'You haven't even seen the gardens. Come, and I'll show them to you.'

Hubert would have preferred to walk with her through these ornamental swards; and he liked the espalier apple-trees with which the garden was divided better than the glare and heat of the greenhouses into which she took him.

' Do you care for flowers ? '

' Not very much.'

'These are all my flowers,' she said, pointing to
many rows of flower-pots. 'Those are Julia's. You
see I run a line of thread around mine, so that there
shall be no mistake. She is not nearly so careful as I
am, and it isn't nice to find that the plants you have
been tending for weeks have been spoilt by over-
watering. I don't say she doesn't love them, but she
forgets them. . . . Just look at those; they are
devoured by insects. They want to be taken out and
given a thorough cleansing. Even then I doubt if
they would come out right,—a plant never forgives
you; it is just like a human being.'

' And doesn't a human being ever forgive ? '

' Oh, I didn't mean that ! ' she said, blushing ; ' but
sometimes I could cry over the poor plants which she
neglects. I daresay you will think me very ridiculous,
but I do cry sometimes, and sometimes I cannot resist taking them out on the sly, and giving them a
thoroughly good syringing,—only you must not tell
her ; we have agreed not to touch each other's flowers.
But I cannot bear to see the poor things dying. How
do we know that they do not suffer ? '

' I don't think it probable.'

'But we don't know for certain,' she said, fixing
her great eyes on him. 'Do we?'

'We know nothing for certain,' he answered; and
then he said, 'You and Mrs. Bentley have lived a
long time together?'

'No; not very long. About a couple of years. I
was about thirteen when I came to Ashwood. I am
now eighteen. Mrs. Bentley is a sort of connection.
She is very poor—that is why Mr. Burnett asked her
to come and live here; besides, as I grew up I wanted
a companion. She has been very good to me. We
have been very happy together—at least, as happy as
one may be; for I don't think that any one is ever very
happy. Have you been very happy?'

'I have not always been happy. But tell me more
about Mrs. Bentley.'

'There is little more to tell. I naturally love her
very much. She nursed me when I was ill—and I'm
often ill; she taught me all I know; she cheered me
when I was sad—when I thought my heart would
break; when everybody else seemed unkind she was
kind. Besides, I could not remain here without her.'
Emily lowered her eyes, and the conversation seemed
to pause.

'I have arranged all that,' Hubert answered

hurriedly. 'I spoke to her last night, and she has consented to remain.'

'That is very good of you.' Emily raised her eyes and looked shyly at Hubert; and then, as if doubtful of herself, she said, 'Do you like her? I'm sure you do. Every one does. Do you not think she is very handsome?'

'I think her an exceedingly pleasant woman, and I'm sure we shall all get on very well together.'

'But don't you think her very handsome?'

'Yes; she is a handsome woman.'

Nothing more was said. Emily drew meditatively on the gravel with the point of her parasol. The gardeners looked up from their work.

'I have to go now,' she said, raising her eyes timidly, 'to feed the swans. You would not care to go so far?'

'On the contrary, I should like it, of all things. A walk by the water on a day like this will be quite a treat.'

'Then will you wait a moment? I will go and fetch the bread.' She returned soon after with a small basket; and a large retriever, tied up in the corner of the yard, barked and lugged at his chain. 'He knows where I am going, and is afraid I shall forget him—aren't you,

dear old Don ? You wouldn't like to miss a walk with
your mistress, would you, dear?' The dog bounded
and rushed from side to side ; it was with difficulty that
Emily loosed him. Once free, he galloped down the
drive, returning at intervals for a caress and a sniff at
the basket which his mistress carried. 'There's nothing there for you, my beautiful Don !'

The drive sloped from the house down to the artificial water, passing under some large elms ; and in the
twilight of the branches where the sunlight played,
and the silence was tremulous with wings, Hubert felt
that Emily had forgiven him. She wore the same
black dress that he had admired her in the night before ; her waist was confined by the same black band ;
but the chestnut hair seemed more beautiful beneath
the black silk sunshade, leaned so gracefully, the black
handle held between thumb and forefinger. And the
little black figure seemed a part of the beautiful
English park, now so green and fragrant in all the flower
and sunlight of June, and decorated with a blue
summer sky, and white clouds moving lazily over the
tops of the trees. And the impression of the beautiful
park was enforced by its reflection, which lay, with the
mute magic of reflected things, in the still water, stirred
only when, with exquisite motion of webbed feet, the

swans propelled their freshness to and fro, balancing themselves in the current where they knew the bread must surely fall.

'They are waiting for me. Cannot you see their black eyes turned towards the bridge?' And she threw the bread from the basket, and the beautiful birds unbent their curved necks, devouring it voraciously under the water.

In the larger portion of this artificial lake there were two islands, thickly wooded. In the smaller, which lay behind Emily and Hubert, there was one small island covered with reeds and low bushes, and this was a favourite haunt for the waterfowl, which now came swimming forward, not daring to approach too near the dangerous swans.

'These are my friends,' said Emily. 'They will follow me to the other end, and I shall be able to feed them as we walk along the meadow.'

Don and Dandy bounded through the tall grass; sometimes foolishly giving chase to the birds that rose up out of the golden grasses, barking in mad eagerness—sometimes pursuing a hare into the distant woods. The last chase had led them far, and both dogs returned panting to walk till they recovered breath by their mistress's side; and to satisfy the retriever's

affection Emily held one hand to him. Playing gently
with his ears, she said—

'Did you ever see much of Mr. Burnett?'

'Not since I was a boy, ten or twelve years ago, when
I was at the University. There was absolutely no
reason for his doing what he did.'

'Yes; there was,' she said in a strangely decisive
tone.

'May I ask——'

'I do not know if I ought to tell you. It would be
better not to. You know,' she continued, speaking
now with a nervous tremor in her voice, 'that I
do not want you to think that I am so very disappointed. I do not know that I am disappointed
at all. You have acted so generously, and it will be
pleasanter to live here with you than with that old
man.'

The conversation fell; but the sweet meadow seemed
to induce confidences, and they were so happy in their
youth and the sorcery of the sunshine. 'Five years
ago I wrote to him,' said Hubert, speaking very slowly,
'asking him to lend me fifty pounds, and he refused.
Since then I have not heard from him.' At the end of
a long silence, the girl said—

'So long as you know that I am no longer angry

with him for having disinherited me, I do not mind
telling you the reason. Two months before he died
he asked me to marry him, and I refused.'

They walked several yards without speaking.

'Do you not think I was right? I was only eighteen,
and he was over sixty.'

'It seems to me quite shocking that he could have
even.contemplated such a thing.'

'But look at these poor ducks; they have followed
us all the way, and I have forgotten to feed them!'
Taking out all the bread that remained in the basket,
Emily threw it to the ducks that had collected where
the dammed-up stream that filled the lake trickled over
a wooden sluice. There was a plank by which to
cross the deep cutting. Hubert and Emily paused,
and stood gazing at the large beech wood that swept
over some rising ground. Don had not been seen for
some time, and they both shouted to him. Presently
a black mass was seen bounding through the flowers,
and the panting animal once more ensconced himself
by his mistress's side.

'I was very fond of Mr. Burnett,' she said, 'but I
could not marry him. I could not marry any man I
did not love.'

'And because you refused to marry him, he did

not mention you in his will. I never heard of such selfishness before!'

'Men are always selfish,' she said sententiously. 'But it really does not matter; things are just the same; he hasn't succeeded in altering anything—at least, not for the worse. We shall get on very well together.'

The conversation paused. Then Emily went on: 'You won't tell any one I told you? I only told you because I did not want you to think me selfish. I was afraid that after the foolish way I behaved last night you might think I hated you. Indeed, I do not. Perhaps everything has happened for the best. I was very fond of the old man. I gave him my whole heart; no father ever had a daughter more attached; but I could not marry him. And it was the remembrance of my love for him that made me burst out crying. I do not think I realised until I saw you how cruelly I had been treated. But you won't tell any one? You won't tell Mrs. Bentley? She knows, of course; but do not tell her that I told you. I do not care that my feelings should be made a subject of discussion. You promise me?'

'I promise you.'

They had now reached the tennis-lawn. The gong

sounded, and Emily said, 'That is lunch, and we shall find Julia waiting for us in the dining-room.' It was as she said. Mrs. Bentley was standing by the sideboard, her basket of keys in her hand; she had not quite finished her housekeeping, and was giving some last instructions to the butler. Hubert noticed that the place at the head of the table was for him, and he sat down a little embarrassed, to carve a chicken. So much home after so many years of homelessness seemed strange.

XI

ON the third day, as soon as breakfast was over, Hubert introduced the subject of his departure. Julia waited, but as Emily did not speak, she said, 'We thought you liked the country better than town.'

'So I do, but——'

'He's tired of us, and we had better leave,' Emily said, abruptly.

Hubert started a little; he looked appealingly at Julia, and seeing the look of genuine pain upon his face, she took pity on him. 'You should not speak like that, Emily.dear; I can see that you pain Mr. Price very much.'

'I hope, Emily, that you will stay here as long as you like,' he said, in a low, gentle voice; 'as long as it is convenient and agreeable to you.'

'We cannot stay here without you,' Emily replied; 'we are your guests.'

'And,' said Julia, smiling, 'if there are guests, there must be a host. But if you have business in London, of course you must go.'

'I was not thinking of myself,' said Hubert, 'but of you ladies. I was afraid that you were already tired of me; that you might like to be left alone; that you had business, preparations. I daresay I was all wrong; but if Emily knew——'

'I'm sorry, Hubert; I did not mean to offend you. I'm very unlucky. You'll forgive me.'

'I've nothing to forgive; I only hope that you'll never think again that I want to get rid of you. I hope that you'll stop at Ashwood as long as ever it suits you to do so. I don't see how I can say more.'

'I like to stop here as long as you are here,' Emily said, in a low voice. 'That is all I meant.'

'Then we're all of one mind, I don't want to go back to London. If you don't find me in your way, I shall be delighted to stay.'

'Of course,' said Julia, 'we poor country folk can hardly hope to amuse you.'

'I don't know about that!' exclaimed Emily. 'Where would he find any one to play and sing to him in the evenings as you can?'

The conversation paused, and all were happier that morning, though none knew why. Days passed, desultory and sweet, and with a pile of books about him, he lay in a long cane chair under the trees; then the book would drop on his knees, and blowing smoke in curling wreaths, he lost himself in dramatic meditations. It was pleasant to see that Emily had grown innocently, childishly fond of her cousin, and her fondness expressed itself in a number of pretty ways. 'Now, Hubert, Hubert, get out of my way,' she would say, feigning a charming petulance ; or she would come and drag him out of his chair, saying, 'Come, Hubert, I can't allow you to lie there any longer; I have to go to South Water, and want you to come with me?'

And walking together, they seemed like an Italian greyhound and a tall, shaggy setter.

A cloud only appeared on Emily's face when Julia spoke of their departure. Julia had proposed that they should leave at the end of the month, and Emily had consented to this arrangement. The end of the month had appeared to her indefinitely distant, but three weeks of the subscribed time had passed, and signs of departure had become more numerous and more peremptory. Allusion had been made to the laundress, and Julia had asked Emily if she could get all her things into a single box; if not, they would have to send to Brighton for another. Emily had no notion of what her box would hold, and she showed little disposition to count her dresses or put her linen in order.

She seemed entirely taken up thinking what books, what pictures, what china she could take away. She would like to have this bookcase, and might she not take the wardrobe from her own room? and she had known the clock all her life, and it did seem so hard to part with it.

'My dear girl, all these things belong to Mr. Price; you really cannot take them away without asking him.'

'But he won't refuse; he'll let me have anything I like.'

'He can't very well refuse, so I think it would be nicer on your part not to ask for anything.'

'I must have some of these things : I want to make the house we are going to live in, in London, look as much like Ashwood as possible.'

'You'd like to take the whole house with you if you could.'

'Yes; I think I should.' And Emily turned and looked vaguely up and down the passage. 'I wonder if he'd give me the picture of the windmill?'

'The landing would look very bare without it.'

'It would indeed, and when we came down here on a visit—for I suppose we shall come down here sometimes on visits—I should miss the picture dreadfully, so I don't think I'll ask him for it. But I must take some pictures away with me. There are a lot of old things in the lumber-room at the top of the house, that no one knows anything about. I think I'll ask him to let me have them. I'll take him for a good long ramble through the house. He hasn't seen any of it yet, except just the rooms we live in down-stairs.'

Emily went straight to Hubert. He was lying in the long wicker chair, his straw hat drawn over his eyes, for the sun was finding its sharp, white way through the leaves of the beeches.

'Now, Hubert, I want you. Are you asleep?'

'Asleep! No, I was only thinking.' He threw his legs over the edge of the low chair and stood up.

'If I tell you what I want, you won't refuse me, will you?'

'No,' he said smilingly; 'I don't think I shall.'

'Are you sure?' she said, looking at him enigmatically. Then in a lighter tone: 'I want you to give me a lot of things—oh, not a great many, nothing very valuable, but——'

'But what, Emily? . . . You can have anything you want.'

'Well, we shall see. You must come with me; I must show you what—I shan't want them unless you like to give them. Come along. Oh, you must come.

138

I should not care about them unless you came with me, and let me point them out.' She passed her little hand into the arm of his rough coat, and led him towards the house. 'You know nothing of your own house, so before I go I intend to show you all over it. You have no idea what a funny old place it is up-stairs —endless old lumber-rooms which you would never think of going into if I didn't take you. When I was a little girl I wasn't often allowed down-stairs : the top of the house still seems to me more real than any other part.' Throwing open a door at the head of the stairs, she said : ' This used to be my nursery. It is all bare and deserted now, but I remember it quite different. I used to spend hours looking out of that window. From it you can see all over the park, and the park used to be my great delight. I used to sit there and make resolutions that next time I went out I would be braver, and explore the hollows full of bushes and tall ferns.'

' Did you never break your resolutions ? '

'Sometimes. I was afraid of meeting fairies or elves. There are glades and hollows that used to seem very wonderful. And they still seem very wonderful, only not quite in the same way. Doesn't the world seem very wonderful to you ? I'm always wondering at things.

But I know I'm only a silly little girl, and yet I like
to talk to you about my fancies. Down there in the
beech wood there is a beautiful glade. I loved to play
there better than anywhere else. I used to lie there on
a fur rug and play at paper dolls. I always fancied
myself a duchess or a princess.'

'You are full of dreams, Emily.'

'Yes; I suppose I am. Everything is pleasant and
happy in dreams. I love dreaming. They thought
I'd never learn to read; but it wasn't because I was
stupid, but because I wouldn't study. I'd put my
hands to my head, and, looking at the book, which I
didn't see, I'd think of all sorts of things, imagine
myself a fairy princess.'

'And it was in this room that you dreamed all those
dreams?'

'Yes; in this dear old room. You see that picture:
that is one of the things I intended to ask you to give
me.'

'What? That old, dilapidated print?'

'You mustn't abuse my picture. I used to spend
hours wondering if those horsemen galloping so madly
through the wood were robbers, and if they had robbed
the castle shown between the trees. I used to wonder
if they would succeed in escaping. They wouldn't

gallop their horses like that unless they were being pursued. . . . Can I have the picture ? '

' Of course you can. Is that—that is not all you are going to ask me for ?'

' I did think of asking you for a few more things. Do you mind ? '

' No, not the least. The more you ask for, the more I shall be pleased.'

' Then you must come down-stairs.'

They went down to the next landing. Emily stopped before a bed-room, and, looking at Hubert shyly and interrogatively, she said—

' This is my room. I don't know if it is in a fit state to show you. I 'm not a very tidy girl. I 'll look first.'

' Yes ; it will do,' she said, drawing back. ' You can look in. I want you to give me that wardrobe. It isn't a very handsome one, but I 've used it ever since I was a little girl ; it has a hollow top, and I used to hide things there. Do you think you can spare it ? '

' Yes ; I think I can,' he said, smiling.

Then she led him up-stairs through the old lumber ·rooms, picking out here and there some generally broken and always worthless piece of furniture, plead- ing for it timidly, and strangely delighted when he

nodded, granting her every request. She asked him to
pull out what she had chosen from the *débris*, and a
curious collection they made in the passage—dim and
worm-eaten pictures, small book-cases, broken vases
which she proposed mending.

Hubert wiped the dust from his hands and coat-
sleeves.

'What a lot of things you have given me! Now
we shall be able to get on nicely with our furnishing.'

'What furnishing?'

'The furnishing of the little house in London where
Julia and I are going to live. You said you intended
to add a hundred a year to the three hundred a year
which Mr. Burnett should have left me; I don't see
why you should do such a thing, but if you do we shall
have four hundred a year to live upon. Julia says that
we shall then be able to afford to give fifty pounds a
year for a house. We can get a very nice little house,
she says, for that—of course, in one of the suburbs.
The great expense will be the furnishing; we are going
to do it on the hire system. I daresay one can get
very nice things in that way, but I do want to make
the place look a little like Ashwood; that is why I'm
asking you for these things. I was always fond of
playing in these old lumber-rooms, and these dim old

pictures, which I don't think any one knows anything of except myself, will remind me of Ashwood. They will look very well, indeed, hanging round our little dining-room. You are sure you don't want them, do you ?'

'No ; I won't want them. I 'm only too pleased to be able to give them to you.'

'You are very good, indeed you are. Look at these old haymakers ; I never saw but one little corner of this picture before ; it was stowed away behind a lot of lumber, and I hadn't the strength to pull it out. . . . I 'm afraid you 've got yourself rather dusty.'

'Oh no ; it will brush off.'

'I shall hang this picture over the fireplace; it will look very well there. I daresay you don't see anything in it, but I 'd sooner have these pictures than those down-stairs. I love the picture of the windmill on the first landing——'

''Then why not have it ? I 'll have it taken down at once.'

' No; I could not think of taking it. How would the landing look without.it ? I should miss it dreadfully when I came here—for I daresay you will ask us to visit you occasionally, when you are lonely, won't you ?'

'My dear Emily, whenever you like, I hope you will come here.'

'And you will come and stay with us in London? Your room will be always ready; I'll look after that. We shall feel very offended, indeed, if you ever think of going to an hotel. Of course, you mustn't expect much; we shall only be able to keep one servant, but we shall try to make you comfortable, and, when you come, you'll take me to the theatres, to see one of your own plays.'

'If my play's being played, certainly. But would it be right for me to pay you visits in London?'

'They would be very wicked people indeed who saw anything wrong in it; you are my cousin. But why do you say such things? You destroy all my pleasure, and I was so happy just now.'

'I'm afraid, Emily, your happiness hangs on a very slender thread.'

She looked at him inquiringly, but feeling that it would be unwise to attempt an explanation, he said in a different tone—

'But, Emily, if you love Ashwood so well, why do you go away?'

'Why do I go away? We have been here now some time. . . . I can't live here always.'

'Why not? Why not let things go on just as they are?'

'And live here with you, I and Julia?'

'Yes; why not?'

'We should bore you; you want to write your plays, you'd get tired of me.'

'Your being here would not prevent my writing my plays. I have been thinking all the while of asking you to remain, but was afraid you would not care to live here.'

'Not care to live here! But you'll get tired of us; we might quarrel.'

'No; we shall never quarrel. You will be doing me a great favour by remaining. Just fancy living alone in this great house, not a soul to speak to all day! I'm sure I should end by going out and hanging myself on one of those trees.'

'You wouldn't do that, would you?'

Hubert laughed. 'You and Mrs. Bentley will be doing me a great favour by remaining. If you go away I shall be robbed right and left, the gardens will go to rack and ruin, and when you come down here you won't know the place, and then, perhaps, we shall quarrel.'

'I shouldn't like Ashwood to go to rack and ruin—

and my poor flowers! And I'm sure you'd forget to feed the swans. If you did that, I could not forgive you.'

'Well, let these grave considerations decide you to remain.'

' Are you really serious?'

' I never was more serious in my life.'

' Well then, may I run and tell Julia?'

'Certainly, and I'll—no, I won't. I'll look up the housemaids and tell them to restore this interesting collection of antiquities to their original dust.'

.

XII

He was, perhaps, a little too conscious of his happiness; and he feared to do anything that would endanger the pleasure of his present life. It seemed to him like a costly thing which might slip from his hand or be broken; and day by day he appreciated more and more the delicate comfort of this well-ordered house— its brightness, its ample rooms, the charm of space within and without, the health of regular and wholesome meals, the presence of these two women, whose first desire was to minister to his least wish or caprice. These, the first spoilings he had received, combined to render him singularly happy. Bohemianism, he often thought, had been forced upon him—it was not natural to him, and though spiritual belief was dead, he experienced in church a resurrection of influences which misfortune had hypnotised, but which were stirring again into life. He was conscious again of this revival of his early life in the evenings when Mrs. Bentley went to the piano; and when playing a game of chess or draughts, remembrances of the old Shropshire rectory came back, sudden, distinct, and sweet. In these days the disease of fame and artistic achievement only sang monotonously, plaintively, like the wind in the valleys where the wind never wholly rests.

Sometimes, when moved by the novel he was reading, he would discuss its merits and demerits with the two women who sat by him in the quiet of the dim drawing-room, their work on their knees, thinking of him. In the excitement of criticism his thoughts wandered to his own work, and the women's eyes filled with reveries, and their hands folded languidly over their knees. He spoke without emphasis, his words seeming to drop from the thick obsession of his dream. At ten the ladies gathered up their work, bade him good-night; and nightly these good-nights grew tenderer, and nightly they went up-stairs more deeply penetrated with a sense of their happiness. But at heart he was a man's man. He hardly perceived life from a woman's point of view; and in the long evenings which he spent with these women he sometimes had to force himself to appear interested in their conversation. He was as far removed from one as from the other. Emily's wilfulness puzzled him, and he did not seem to have anything further to talk about to Mrs. Bentley.

He missed the bachelor evenings of former days—
the whisky and water, the pipes, and the literary discussion; and as the days went by he began to think
of London; his thoughts turned affectionately towards
the friends he had not seen for so long, and at the
end of July he announced his intention of running
up to town for a few days. So one morning breakfast was hurried through; Emily was sure there was
plenty of time; Hubert looked at the clock and said
he must be off; Julia ran after him with parcels
which he had forgotten; farewell signs were waved;
the dog-cart passed out of sight, and, after lingering
a moment, the women returned to the drawing-room
thoughtfully.

'I wonder if he'll catch the train,' said Emily,
without taking her face from the window.

'I hope so; it will be very tiresome for him if he
has to come back. There isn't another train before
three o'clock.'

'If he missed this train he wouldn't go until to-
morrow morning. . . . I wonder how long he'll stay
away. Supposing something happened, and he never
came back!' Emily turned round and looked at Julia
in dreamy wonderment.

'Not come back at all? What nonsense you are

talking, Emily! He won't be away more than a fortnight or three weeks.'

'Three weeks! that seems a very long while. How
shall we get through our evenings?'

Emily had again turned towards the window. Julia
did not trouble to reply. She smiled a little, as she
paused on the threshold, for she remembered that no
more than a few weeks ago Emily had addressed to her
passionate speeches declaring her to be her only friend,
and that they would like to live together, content in
each other's companionship, always ignoring the rest
of the world. Although she had not mistaken these
speeches for anything more than the nervous passion
of a moment, the suddenness of the recantation surprised her a little. Three or four days after, the girl
was in a different mood, and when they came into
the drawing-room after dinner she threw her arms
about Julia's neck, saying, 'Isn't this like old times?
Here we are, living all alone together, and I'm not
boring myself a bit. I never shall have another friend
like you, Julia.'

'But you'll be very glad when Hubert comes back.'

'There's no harm in that, is there? I should be
very ungrateful if I wasn't. Think how good he has
been to us. . . I'm afraid you don't like him, Julia.'

'Oh, yes, I do, Emily.'

'Not so much as I do.' And raising herself—she
was sitting on Julia's knees—Emily looked at Julia.

'Perhaps not,' Julia replied, smiling; 'but then I
never hated him as much as you did.'

A cloud came over Emily's face. 'I did hate him,
didn't I? You remember that first evening? You
remember when you came up-stairs and found me
trembling in the passage—I was afraid to go to bed.
. . . I begged you to allow me to sleep with you.
You remember how we listened for his footstep in
the passage, as he went up to bed, and how I clung
to you? Then the dreams of that night. I never
told you what my dreams were, but you remember
how I woke up with a cry, and you asked me what
was the matter?'

'Yes, I remember.'

'I dreamt I was with him in a garden, and was
trying to get away; but he held me by a single hair,
and the hair would not break. How absurd dreams
are! And the garden was full of flowers, but every
time I tried to gather them, he pulled me back by
that single hair. I don't remember any more, only
something about running wildly away from him, and
losing myself in a dark forest, and there the ground

was soft like a bog, and it seemed as if I were going
to be swallowed up every moment. It was a terrible
sensation. All of a sudden I woke with a cry. The
room was grey with dawn, and you said: "Emily
dear, what have you been dreaming, to cry out like
that?" I was too tired and frightened to tell you
much about my dream, and next morning I had forgotten it. I did not remember it for a long time
after, but all the same some of it came true. Don't
you remember how I met Hubert next morning on
the lawn? We went into the garden and spent the
best part of the morning walking about the lake. . . .
I don't know if I told you—I ran away when I heard
him coming, and should have got away had it not
been for this tiresome dog. He called after me, using
my Christian name. I was so angry I think I hated
him then more than ever. We walked a little way,
and the next thing I remember was thinking how nice
he was. I don't know how it all happened. Now I
think of it, it seems like magic. It was the day that
my old donkey ran away with the mowing machine
and broke the flower-vase, the dear old thing; we
had a long talk about "Jack." And then I took
Hubert into the garden and showed him the flowers.
I don't think he cares much about flowers; he pre-

tended, but I could see it was only to please me. Then I knew that he liked me, for when I told him I was going to feed the swans, he said he loved swans and begged to be allowed to come too. I don't think a man would say that if he didn't like you, do you ?'

Emily's mind seemed to contain nothing but memories of Hubert. What he had said on this occasion, how he had looked at her on another. The conversation paused and Emily sunned herself in the enchantment of recollection, until at last breaking forth again, she said—

'Have you noticed how Ethel Eastwick goes after him ? And the odd part of it is, that she can't see that he dislikes her. He thinks nothing of her singing ; he remained talking to me in the conservatory the whole time. I asked him to come into the drawing-room, but he pretended to misunderstand me, and asked me if I felt a draught. He said, "Let me get you a shawl." I said, "I assure you, Hubert, I don't feel any draught." But he would not believe me, and said he could not allow me to sit there without something on my shoulders. I begged of him not to move, for I knew that Ethel would never forgive me if I interrupted her singing; but he said he could get me a wrap without interrupting any one. He opened the conservatory door, ran across the lawn round to the front door, and came back with—what do you think? With two wraps instead of one; one was mine, and the other belonged to—I don't know who it belonged to. So I said, "Oh, what ever shall we do? I cannot let you go back again. If any one was to come in and find me alone, what ever would they think!" Hubert said, "Will you come with me? A walk in the garden will be pleasanter than sitting in the conservatory." I didn't like going at first, but I thought there couldn't be much harm.'

It seemed to Emily very terrible and very wonderful, and she experienced throughout her numbed sense a strange, thrilling pain, akin to joy, and she sat, her little fragile form lost in the arm-chair, her great eyes fixed in ecstasy, seeing still the dark garden with the great star risen like a phantom above the trees. That evening had been to her a wonder and an enchantment, and her pausing thoughts dwelt on the moment when the distant sound of a bell reached their ears, and the bell came nearer, clanging fiercely in the sonorous garden. Then they saw a light—some one had come for them with a lantern—a joke, a suitable pleasantry, and amid joyous laughter, watching the setting moon,

they had gone back to the tiled house, where dancers
still passed the white-curtained windows. Hubert had
sat by her at supper, serving her with meat and drink.
In the sway of memory she trembled and started,
looking in the great arm-chair like a little bird that
the moon keeps awake in its soft nest. She no longer
wished to tell Julia of that night in the garden; her
sensation of it lay far beyond words.; it was her
secret, and it shone through her dreamy youth even
as the star had shone through the heavens that night.
Suddenly she said—

'I wonder what Hubert is doing in London? I
wonder where he is now?'

'Now? It is just nine. I suppose he's in some
theatre.'

'I suppose he goes a great deal to the theatre. I
wonder who he goes with. He has lots of friends in
London—actresses, I suppose; he knows them who
play in his plays. He dines at his club——'

'Or at a restaurant.'

'I wonder what a restaurant is like; ladies dine at
restaurants, don't they?'

As Julia was about to make reply, the servant
brought her a letter. She opened the envelope, and
took out a long, closely-written letter; she turned it

over to see the signature, and then looking toward
Emily, she said, with a pleasant smile—

'Now I shall be able to answer your questions better;
this letter is from Mr. Price.'

'Oh, what does he say? Read it.'

'Wait a moment, let me glance through it first; it is
very difficult to read.' A few moments after, Julia
said, 'There's not much that would interest you in
the letter, Emily; it is all about his play. He says he
would have written before if he had not been so
busy looking out for a theatre, and engaging actors
and actresses. He hopes to start rehearsing next
week.

"I say I hope, because there are still some parts of the
play which do not satisfy me, particularly the third act. I
intend to work steadily on the play till next Thursday, five
or six hours every day; I am in perfect health and spirits,
and ought to be able to get the thing right. Should I fail
to satisfy myself, or should any further faults appear when
we begin to rehearse the piece, I shall dismiss my people,
pack up my traps, and return to Ashwood. There I shall
have quiet; here, people are continually knocking at my
door, and I cannot deny my friends the pleasure of seeing
me, if that is a pleasure. But at Ashwood, as I say, I shall
be sure of quiet, and can easily finish the play this autumn,
and February is a better time than September to produce
a play."'

'Then he goes on,' said Julia, 'to explain the alterations he contemplates making. There's no use reading
you all that.'

'I suppose you think I should not understand.'

'My dear Emily, if you want to read the letter, there
it is.'

'I don't want to see your letter.'

'What do you mean, Emily?'

'Nothing, only I think it rather strange that he didn't
write to me.'

Some days after, Emily took up the book that Julia
had laid down. '"Shakespeare's Plays." I suppose
you are reading them so that you'll be able to talk to
him better.'

'I never thought of such a thing, Emily.' At the
end of a long silence Emily said—

'Do you think clever men like clever women?'

'I don't know. Some say they do, some say they
don't. I believe that really clever men, men of genius,
don't.'

'I wonder if Hubert is a man of genius. What do
you think?'

'I really am not capable of expressing an opinion on
the matter.'

Another week passed away, and Emily began to

assume an air of languor and timid yearning. One
day she said—

'I wonder he doesn't write. He hasn't answered my
letter yet. Has he answered yours?'

'He has not written to me again. He hasn't time
for letter-writing. He is working night and day at his
play.'

'I suppose he'd never think of coming down by the
morning train. He'd be sure to come by the five
o'clock.'

'He won't come without writing. He'd be sure to
write for the dog-cart.'

'I suppose so. There's no use in looking out for
him.'

But, notwithstanding her certitude on the point,
Emily could not help choosing five o'clock as the
time for a walk, and Julia noticed that the girl's feet
seemed to turn instinctively towards the lodge. Often
she would leave the flowers she was tending on the
terrace, and stand looking through the dim, sun-smitten
landscape toward the red-brown spot, which was Southwater, in the middle of the long plain.

XIII

HUBERT felt called upon to entertain his friends, and one evening they all sat dining at Hurlingham in the long room. The conversation, as usual, had been about books and pictures.

It was the moment when strings of lanterns were hoisted from tree to tree. In front of a large space of sky the coloured globes were crude and trivial; but in the shadows of the trees by the river, where the mist rose into the branches, they had begun to awaken the first impression of melancholy and the sadness of *fête*. It was the moment when the great trees hung heavy and motionless, strangely green and solemn beneath a slate-coloured sky; and the plaintive waltz cried on Hungarian fiddle-strings, till it seemed the soul of this feminine evening. The fashionable crowd had moved out upon the lawn; the white dresses were phantom blue, and the men's coats faded into obscure masses, darkening the gathering shadows. It was the moment when voices soften, and every heart, overpowered with yearning, is impelled to tell of grief and disillusion; and every moment the wail of the fiddles grew more unbearable, tearing the heart to its very depths.

Author and actor-manager walked up the lawn puffing at their cigars. The others sat watching, knowing that the opportunity had come for criticism of their friend.

'He does not change much,' said Harding. 'Circumstances haven't affected him. A year ago he lived in a garret re-writing his play *Divorce*. He now rewrites *Divorce* in a handsome house in Sussex.'

'I thought he had finished his play,' said Thompson. 'I heard that he was going to take a theatre and produce it himself.'

'But did you not hear him say at dinner that he was re-writing as he rehearsed? I met one of the actors yesterday. He doesn't know what to make of it. He gets a new part every week to learn.'

'Do you think he'll ever produce it?'

'I doubt it. At the last moment he'll find that the third act doesn't satisfy him, and will postpone the production till the spring.'

'What do you think of his work?'

'Very intelligent, but a little insipid—like himself. Look at him. *Il est bien l'homme de ses ouvres*. There is something dry about him, and his writings are like himself—hard, dry and wanting in personal passion.'

'Yet he talks charmingly, with vivacity and intelligence, and he is so full of appreciation of Shakespeare, Goethe, and such genuine love for antiquity.'

'I've heard him talk Shakespeare, Goethe, and Ibsen,' said Harding, 'but I never heard him say anything new, anything personal. It seems to me that you mistake quotation for perception. He assimilates, but he originates nothing. He has read a great deal; he is covered with literature like a rock with moss and lichen. He's appreciative, I will say that for him. He would make a capital editor, or a tutor, or a don, an Oxford don. He would be perfectly happy as a don; he could read up the German critics and expound Sophocles. He would be perfectly happy as a don. As it is, he is perfectly miserable.'

'There was a fellow who had a studio over mine,' said Thompson. 'He had been in the army and used to paint a bit. The academy by chance hung a portrait, so he left the army and turned portrait-painter. One day he saw a picture by Velasquez, and he understood how horrid were the red things he used to send to the academy. He used to come down to see me; he used to say, "I wish I had never seen a picture, by

161   L

Gad, it is driving me out of my mind." Poor chap, I
wanted him to go back to the army. I said, Why paint?
no one forces you to; it makes you miserable; don't do
so any more. When you have anything to say, art is a
joy; when you haven't, it is a curse to yourself and to
others.'

Philipps, the editor of *The Cosmopolitan*, turned
towards Harding, and he said—

'I cannot follow you in your estimate of Hubert
Price. I don't see him either mentally or physically
as you do. It seems to me that you distort the facts
to make them fit in with your theory. He is tall and
thin, but I do not think that his nature is hard and dry.
I should, on the contrary, say that he was of a soft
rather than a hard nature. The expression of his face
is mild and melancholy. I do not detect the dry, hard,
rocky basis of which you speak. I should say that
Price was a sentimental man.'

'I have never heard of him being in love,' said
Harding. 'I should say that he had been entirely un-
influenced by women.'

'But love of women is only one form of sentiment-
ality and not the highest, nor the deepest,' said Philipps.
'I can imagine a man being exceedingly sentimental
and not caring about women at all.'

'What you say is true,' said Harding. His face showed that he felt the observation to be true and was interested in it. 'But I think I described him truly when I said he was like a rock overgrown with moss and lichen. There is not sufficient root-hold for any idea to grow in him, it withers and dies. Examine his literature, and you'll see it is as I say. He has written some remarkable plays, I don't say he hasn't. But they seem to be better than they are. He gets a picturesque situation, but there is always something mechanical about it. There's a human emotion somewhere, but it's never really there ; it might have been, but it is not. . . . It is very well done, it is very intelligent ; but it does not seem to live, to palpitate. . . . In like manner there are men who have read everything, who understand everything, who can theorise ; they can tell you all about the masterpiece, but when it comes to producing one, well, they're not on in that scene.'

'What an excellent character he would make in a novel! A drama of sterility,' said Phillips.

'Or the dramas which they bring about,' said Harding.

'Yes, or the dramas they bring about. But what drama can Price bring about—he shuts himself up in a

163

room and tries to write a play,' said Phillips. 'I don't
see how he can dramatise any life but his own.'

'All deviations from the normal tend to bring about
drama,' said Harding.

'Then, why don't you do a Hubert Price in a book?
It would be most interesting. Do you think you ever
will?'

'I don't think so.'

'Why not? Because he is a friend of yours, and you
would not like——'

'I never allow my private life to interfere with
my literature. No; for quite other reasons. I admit
that he represents physically and mentally a great
deal of the intellectual impotence current in our time.
But it would be difficult, I think, to bring vividly before
the reader that tall, thin, blonde man, with his pale
gentle eyes and his insipid mind. I should take quite a
different kind of man as my model.'

'What kind of man?' said Phillips, and the five or
six writers and painters leaned forward to listen to
Harding.

'I think I should imagine a man about the medium
height. A nice figure, light, trim, neat. Good-looking, straight nose, eyes bright and intelligent. I think
he would have beard, a very close-cut beard. The

turn of his mind would be metaphysical and poetic—an intense subtility of mind combined with much order. He would be full of little habits. He would have note-books of a special kind in which to enter his ideas. The tendency of his mind would be towards concision, and he would by degrees extend his desire for concision into the twilight and the night of symbolism.'

'A sort of constipated Browning,' said Phillips.

'Exactly,' said Harding.

'And would you have him married?' asked John Norton.

'Certainly. I imagine him living in a tiny little house somewhere near the river—Westminster or Chelsea. His wife would be a dreadful person, thin, withered, herring-gutted—a sort of red herring with a cap. But his daughter would be charming, she would have inherited her father's features. I can imagine these women living in admiration of this man, tending on him, speaking very little, removed from worldly influences, seeing only the young men who come every Tuesday evening to listen to the poet's conversation—I don't hear them saying much—I can see them sitting in a corner listening for the ten thousandth time to æstheticisms not one word of which they understand, and about ten o'clock stealing away to some mysterious chamber. Something of the poet's sterility would have descended upon them.'

'That is how you imagine *un génie raté*,' said Phillips. 'Your conception is clear enough ; why don't you write the book ?'

'Because there is nothing more to say on the subject. It is a subject for a sketch, not for a book. But of this I'm sure, that the dry-rock man would come out more clearly in a book than the soft, insipid, gentle, companionable, red-bearded fellow.'

'If Price were the dry, sterile nature you describe, we should feel no interest in him, we should not be discussing him as we are,' said Phillips.

'Yes, we should—Price suffers ; we're interested in him because he suffers—because he suffers in public—"I never was happy except on those rare occasions when I thought I was a great man." In that sentence you'll find the clew to his attractiveness. But in him there is nothing of the irresponsible passion which is genius. There's that little Rose Massey—that little baby who spends half her day dreaming, and who is as ignorant as a cod-fish. Well, she has got that something —that undefinable but always recognisable something. It was Price who discovered her. We used to laugh at him when he said she had genius. He was right ;

166

we were wrong. The other night I was standing in the wings; she was coming down from her dressing-room—she lingered on the stairs, looking the most insignificant little thing you can well imagine; but the moment her cue came a strange light came into her eyes and a strange life was fused in her limbs; she was transformed, and went on the stage a very symbol of passion and romance.'

The slate colour of the sky did not seem to change, and yet the night grew visibly denser in the park; and there had come the sensation of things ended, a movement of wraps thrown over shoulders and thought of bedtime and home. The crowd was moving away, and nearly lost in the darkness Hubert came towards his friends. He had just knocked the ash from his cigar, and as he drew in the smoke the glow of the lighted end fled over his blonde face.

XIV

ONE day a short letter came from Hubert, asking Mrs. Bentley to send the dog-cart to the station to fetch him. He had decided to come home at once, and postpone the production of his play till the coming spring.

Every rehearsal had revealed new and serious faults of construction. These he had attempted to remove when he went home in the evening, but though he often worked till daybreak, he did not achieve much. The very knowledge that he must come to rehearsal with the re-written scene seemed to produce in him a sort of mental paralysis, and, striking the table with his fist, he would get up, and a thought would cross his mind of how he might escape from this torture. After one terrible night, in which he feared his brain was really giving way, he went down to the theatre and dismissed the company, for he had resolved to return to Ashwood and spend another autumn and another winter re-writing *The Gipsy*. If it did not come right then, he would bother no more about it. Why should he? There was so much else in life besides literature. He had plenty of money, and was determined in any case to enjoy himself. So did his thoughts run as he leaned back on the cushions of a first-class carriage, glancing casually through the evening paper. Presently his eye was caught by a paragraph narrating an odd calamity which had overtaken a scene carpenter, an honest, respectable, sober, hard-working man, who had fulfilled all social obligations as perfectly as the most exacting could desire, until the day he had conceived the idea of a machine for the better exhibition of advertisements on the hoardings. His system was based on the roller-towel. The roller was moved by clockwork, and the advertisements went round like the towel. At first he spent his spare time and his spare money upon it, but as the hobby took possession of him, he devoted all his time and all his money to it; then he pawned his clothes, and then he raised money on the furniture; the brokers came in, and finally the poor fellow was taken to a lunatic asylum, and his wife and family were thrown on the parish. The story impressed Hubert strangely. He saw an analogy between himself and the crazy inventor, and he asked himself if he would go on re-writing *The Gipsy* until he went out of his mind. 'Even if I do,' he thought, 'I can hurt no one but myself. No one else is dependent on me; my hobby can hurt no one but myself.' These forebodings passed away, and his mind filled up with schemes of work. He knew exactly what he wanted to do, and he looked forward to doing it. He wanted quiet, he wanted long days alone with himself. Such were his thoughts in the dog-cart as he drove home, and it was therefore vaguely unpleasant to him to meet the two ladies waiting for him at the lodge gate. Their smiles of welcome irritated him ; he longed for the solitude of his study, the companionship of his work; and instead he had to sit with them in the drawing-room, and tell them how he liked London, what he had done there, whom he had seen there, and why he had been unable to finish his play to his satisfaction.

In the morning Emily or Mrs. Bentley was generally about to pour out his coffee for him and keep him company. One day Hubert noticed that it was no longer Mrs. Bentley but Emily who met him in the passage, and followed him into the dining-room. And while he was eating she sat with her feet on the fender, talking of some girls in the neighbourhood—their jealousies, and how Edith Eastwick could not think of anything for herself, but always copied her dresses. Dandy drowsed at her feet, and very often she would take him to the window and make him go through all his tricks, calling on Hubert to admire him.

She had a knack of monopolising Hubert, and since his return from London, her desire to do so had become almost a determination. Hubert showed no disinclination, and after breakfast they were to be seen together in the gardens. Hubert was a great catch, and there were other young ladies eager to be agreeable to him; but he did not seem to desire flirtation with any. So they came to speak of him as a very clever man, no doubt; but as they knew nothing about plays, he very probably did not care to talk to them. Hubert was not attractive in general society, and he would soon have failed to interest them at all had it not been for Emily. She was proud of her influence over him, and for the first time showed a desire to go into society. Day by day her conversation turned more and more on tennis-parties, and she even spoke about a ball. He consented to take her; and he had to dance with her, and she refused nearly every one, saying she was tired, leading Hubert away for long conversations in the galleries and on the staircases. Hubert had positively nothing to say to her; but she seemed quite happy as long as she was with him. And as they drove through the dawn Emily chattered of a hundred trifles,—what Edith had said, what Mabel wore, of the possibility of a marriage, and the arrival of a detachment of some cavalry regiment. Hubert found it hard to affect interest in these conversations. His brain was weary with waltz tunes, the shape of shoulders, and the glare and rustle of silk; but as she chattered, rubbing the misted windows from time to time, so as to determine how far they were from home, he wondered if he should ever marry, and half playfully he thought of her as his wife.

But without warning his dreams were broken by a sudden thought, and he said—

'Another time, I think it will be better, my dear Emily, that Mrs. Bentley should take you out.'

'Why should you not take me out? . . . I suppose you don't care to—I bore you.'

'No; on the contrary, I enjoy it—I like to see you amused; but I think you should have a proper chaperon.'

Emily did not answer; and a little cloud came over her face. Hubert thought she looked even prettier in her displeasure than she had done in her joy; and he went to sleep thinking of her. Never had he thought her so beautiful—never had she touched him with so

personal an interest; and next morning, when he
lounged in his study, he was glad to hear her knock at
the door; and the half-hour he spent with her there,
yielding to her pleading to come for a walk with her, or
drive her over to Southwater in the dog-cart, was one
of unalloyed pleasure. But a few days after, as he lay
in bed, a new idea came to him for his third act. So
he said he would have breakfast in his study. He
dressed, thinking the whole time how he could round
off his idea and bring it into the act. So clear and
precise did it seem in his mind that he sat down
immediately after breakfast, forgetting even his matu-
tinal cigar, and wrote with a flowing pen. He had
left orders that he was not to be disturbed; and was
annoyed when the door opened and Emily entered.

'I am very sorry, but you must not be cross with
me; I do so want you to come and see the Eastwicks
with me.'

'My dear Emily, I could not think of such a thing.
this morning. I am very busy—indeed I am.'

'What are you doing? Nothing very important, I
can see. You are only writing your play. You might
come with me.'

'My play is as important to me as a visit to the
Eastwicks is to you,' he answered, smiling.

'I have promised Edith. . . . I really do wish you would come.'

'My dear Emily, it is quite impossible : do let me get on with my work !'

Emily's face instantly changed expression ; she turned to leave the room, and Hubert had to go after her and beg her to forgive him—he really had not meant to be rude to her.

'You don't care to talk to me. I am not clever enough for you.'

Then pity took him, and he made amends by suggesting they should go for a walk in the park, and she often succeeded ·in leading him even to dry, uninteresting neighbours. But the burden grew heavier, and soon he could endure no longer the evenings of devotion to her in the drawing-room, where the presence of Mrs. Bentley seemed to fill her with incipient re-bellion. One evening after dinner, as he was about to escape up-stairs, Emily took his arm, pleading that he should play at least one game of backgammon with her. He played three; and then, thinking he had done enough, he took up a novel and began to read. Emily was bitterly offended. She sat in a corner, a picture of deep misery; and whenever he spoke ¡to Mrs. Bentley, he thought she would burst into tears.

It was exasperating to be the perpetual victim of such folly; and, pressed by the desire to talk to Mrs. Bentley about the book he was reading, he suggested that she should come with him to the meet. The Harriers met for the first time that season at not five miles from Ashwood. Mrs. Bentley pleaded an engagement. She had promised to go over to tea at the rectory.

'Oh, we shall be back in plenty of time; I'll leave you at the rectory on our way home.'

'Thank you, Mr. Price; but I do not think I can go.'

'And why, may I ask?'

'Well, perhaps Emily would like to go.'

'Emily has a cold, and it would be folly of her to venture a long drive on a cold morning.'

'My cold is quite well.'

'You were complaining before dinner how bad it was.'

'If you don't want to take me, say so.' Tears were now streaming down her cheeks.

'My dear Emily, I am only too pleased to have you with me; I was only thinking of your cold.'

'My cold is quite gone,' she said, with brightening face; and next morning she came down with her waterproof on her arm, and she had on a new cloth dress which she had just received from London.

Hubert recognised in each article of attire a sign that she was determined to carry her point. It seemed cruel to tell her to take her things off, and he glanced at Mrs. Bentley and wondered if she were offended.

'I hope the drive won't tire you; you know the meet is at least five miles from here.'

Emily did not answer. She looked charming with her great boa tied about her throat, and sprang into the dog-cart all lightness and joy.

'I hope you are well wrapped up about the knees,' said Mrs. Bentley.

'Oh yes, thank you; Hubert is looking after me.'

Mrs. Bentley's calm, statuesque face, whereon no trace of envy appeared, caught Hubert's attention as he gathered up the reins, and he thought how her altruism contrasted with the passionate egotism of the young girl.

'I hope Julia was not disappointed. I know she wanted to come; but——'

'But what?'

'Well, no one likes Julia more than I do, and I don't want to say anything against her; but, having lived so long with her, I see her faults better than you can. She is horribly selfish! It never occurs to her to think of me.'

Hubert did not answer, and Emily looked at him

inquiringly. At last she said, 'I suppose you don't think so?'

'Well, Emily, since you ask me, I must say that I think she took it very good-humouredly. You said you were ill, and it was all arranged that I should drive her to the meet; then you suddenly interposed, and said you wanted to go; and the moment you mentioned your desire to go, she gave way without a word. I really don't know what more you want.'

'You don't know Julia. You cannot read her face. She never forgets anything, and is storing it up, and will pay me out for it sooner or later.'

'My dear Emily, how can you say such things? I never heard—— She is always ready to sacrifice herself for you.'

'You think so. She has a knack of pretending to be more unselfish than another; but she is in reality intensely selfish.'

'All I can say is that it does not strike me so. I never saw any one give way more good-humouredly than she did to-day.'

'I don't think that that is so wonderful, after all. She is only a paid companion; and I do not see why she should go driving about the country with you, and I be left at home.'

Hubert was somewhat shocked. The conversation paused.

'She gets on very well with men,' Emily said at last, breaking an irritating silence somewhat suddenly. 'They say she is very good-looking. Don't you think so?'

'Oh yes, she is certainly a pretty woman—or, I should say, a good-looking woman. She is too. tall to be what one generally understands as a pretty woman.'

'Do you like tall women?'

At that moment the hunt appeared in the field at the bottom of the hill. A grey horse had just got rid of his rider, and after galloping round and round, his head in the air, stopped and began to graze. The others jumped the hedge, and the greater part of the field got over the brook in capital style. Emily and Hubert watched them with delighted eyes, for the sight was indeed picturesque this fine autumn day. Even their horse pricked up his ears and began neighing, and Hubert had to hold him tight in hand, lest he should break away while they were enjoying the spectacle. At that moment a poor little animal, with fear-haunted eyes, and in all the agony of fatigue, appeared above the crest of the hill, and immediately after came the

straining hounds, one within a dozen yards of the poor
little beast, now running in a circle, uttering the most
plaintive and pitiful cries.

'Oh, they are not going to kill it!' cried Emily.
'Oh, save it, save it, Hubert!' She hid her face in her
hands. 'Did it escape? is it killed?' she said, looking
round. 'Oh, it is too cruel!' The huntsman was
calling to the hounds, holding something above them,
and at every moment horses' heads appeared over the
brow of the hill.

There was more hunting; and when the October
night began to gather, and the lurid sunset flared up in
the west, Hubert got out another wrap, and placed it
about Emily's shoulders. But although the chill night
had drawn them close together in the dog-cart, they
were as widely separated as if oceans were between
them. So far as lay in his power he had hidden the
annoyance that the intrusion of her society had
occasioned him ; and, to deceive her, very little con-
cealment was necessary. So long as she saw him she
seemed to live in a dream, unconscious of every other
thought.

They rolled through a gradual effacement of things,
seeing the lights of the farmhouses in the long plain
start into existence, and then remain fixed, like gold

beetles pinned on a blue curtain. The chill evening
drew her to him, till they seemed one ; and full of the
intimate happiness of the senses which comes of a long
day spent in the open air, she chattered of indifferent
things. He thought how pleasant the drive would be
were he with Mrs. Bentley—or, for the matter of that,
with any one with whom he could talk about the novel
that had interested him. They rolled along the smooth
wide road, watching the streak of light growing
narrower in a veil of light grey cloud drawn athwart
the sky. Overpowered by her love, the girl hardly
noticed his silence ; and when they passed through the
night of an overhanging wood her flesh thrilled, and a
little faintness came over her ; for the leaves that
brushed her face had seemed like a kiss from her
lover.

XV

ONE afternoon, about the end of September, Hubert came down from his study about tea-time, and announced that he had written the last scene of his last act. Emily was alone in the drawing-room.

'Oh, how glad I am ! · Then it is done at last. Why not write at once and engage the theatre ? When shall we go to London ? '

'Well, I don't mean that the play could be put into rehearsal to-morrow. It still requires a good deal of overhauling. Besides, even if it were completely finished, I should not care to produce it at once. I should like to lay it aside for a couple of months, and see how it read then.'

'What a lot of trouble you do take ! Does every one who writes plays take so much trouble ? '

'No, I'm afraid they do not, nor is it necessary they should. Their plays are merely incidents strung together more or less loosely ; whereas my play is the development of a temperament, of temperamental

181

characteristics which cannot be altered, having been
inherited through centuries; it must therefore pursue
its course to a fatal conclusion. In Shakespeare——
But no, no! these things have no interest for you.
You shall have the nicest dress that money can buy;
and if the play succeeds——'

The girl raised her pathetic eyes. In truth, she
cared not at all what he talked to her about; she was
occupied with her own thoughts of him, and just to sit
in the room with him, and to look at him occasionally,
was sufficient. But for once his words had pained her.
It was because she could not understand that he did
not care to talk to her. Why did she not understand?
It was hard for a little girl like her to understand such
things as he spoke about; but she would understand;
and then her thoughts passed into words, and she
said—

'I understand quite as well as Julia. She knows
the names of more books than I, and she is very
clever at pretending that she knows more than she
does.'

At that moment Mrs. Bentley entered. She saw
that Emily was enjoying her talk with her cousin, and
tried to withdraw. But Hubert told her that he had
written the last act; she pretended to be looking for a

book, and then for some work which she said had
dropped out of her basket.

'If Emily would only continue the talking,' she
thought, 'I should be able to get away.' But Emily
said not a word. She sat as if frozen in her chair; and
at length Mrs. Bentley was obliged to enter, however
cursorily, into the conversation.

'If you have written out *The Gipsy* from end to end,
I should advise you to produce it without further delay.
Once it is put on the stage, you will be able to see
better where it is wrong.'

'Then it will be too late. The critics will have
expressed their opinion; the work will be judged.
There are only one or two points about which I am
doubtful. I wish Harding were here. I cannot work
unless I have some one to talk to about my work. I
don't mean to say that I take advice; but the very fact
of reading an act to a sympathetic listener helps me.
I wrote the first act of *Divorce* in that way. It was all
wrong. I had some vague ideas about how it might
be mended. A friend came in; I told him my difficulties; in telling them they vanished, and I wrote
an entirely new act that very night.'

'I'm sorry,' said Mrs. Bentley, 'that I am not Mr.
Harding. It must be very gratifying to one's feelings

to be able to help to solve a literary difficulty, particularly if one cannot write oneself.'

'But you can—I'm sure you can. I remember
asking your advice once before; it was excellent, and
was of immense help to me. Are you sure it will not
bore you? I shall be so much obliged if you will.'

'Bore me! No, it won't bore me,' said Mrs. Bentley.
'I'm sure I feel very much flattered.' The colour
mounted to her cheek, a smile was on her lips; but it
went out at the sight of Emily's face.

'Then come up to my study. We shall have just
time to get through the first act before dinner.'

Mrs. Bentley hesitated; and, noticing her hesitation, Hubert looked surprised. At that moment Emily
said—

'May I not come too?'

'Well, I don't know, Emily. You see that we wish
to see if there is anything in the play that a young
girl should not hear.'

'Always an excuse to get rid of me. You want to
be alone. I never come into the room that you do not
stop speaking. Oh, I can bear it no longer!'

'My dear Emily!'

'Don't touch me! Go to her; shut yourself up
together. Don't think of me. I can bear it no

longer!` And she fled from the room, leaving behind her a sensation of alarm and pity. Hubert and Mrs. Bentley stood looking at each other, both at a loss for words. At last he said—

'That poor child will cry herself into her grave. Have you noticed how poorly she is looking?'

'Not noticed! But you do not know half of it. It has been going on now a long time. You don't know half!'

'I have noticed that things are not settling down as I hoped they would. It really has become quite dreadful to see that poor face looking reproachfully at you all day long. And I am quite at a loss to know what's the right thing to do.'

'It is worse than you think. You have not noticed that we hardly speak now?'

'You—who were such friends—surely not!'

Then she told him hurriedly, in brief phrases, of the change that had taken place in Emily in the last three months. 'It was only the other night she accused me of going after you, of having designs upon you. It is very painful to have to tell you these things, but I have no choice in the matter. She lay on her bed crying, saying that every one hated her, that she was thoroughly miserable. Somehow she seems naturally an unhappy child. She was unhappy at home before she came here; but then I believe she had excellent reasons,—her mother was a very terrible person. However, all that is past; we have to consider the present now. She accused me of having designs on you, insisting all the while that every one was talking about it, and that she was fretting solely because of my good name. Of course, it is very ridiculous; but it is very pitiful, and will end badly if we don't take means to put a stop to it. I shouldn't be surprised if she went off her head. We ought to have the best medical advice.'

'This is very serious,' he said. And then, at the end of a long silence, he said again, 'This is very serious—perhaps far more serious than we think.'

'Not more serious than I think. I ought to have spoken about it to you before; but the subject is a delicate one. She hardly sleeps at all at night; she cries sometimes for hours; she works herself up into such fits of nervousness that she doesn't know what she is saying,—accuses me of killing her, and then repents, declaring that I am the only one who has ever cared for her, and begs of me not to leave her. I do assure you it is becoming very serious.'

'Have you any proposal to make regarding her?

I need hardly say that I'm ready to carry out any idea of yours.'

'You know what the cause of it is, I suppose?'

'I do not know; I am not certain. I daresay I'm mistaken.'

'No, you are not; I wish you were—that is to say, unless—— But I was saying that it is most serious. The child's health is affected; she is working herself up into an awful state of mind; she is losing all self-control. I'm sure I'm the last person who would say anything against her; but the time has come to speak out. Well, the other day, when we were at the East-wicks, you took the chair next to mine when she left the room. When she returned, she saw that you had changed your place, and she said to Ethel Eastwick, "Oh, I'm fainting. I cannot go in there; they are together." Ethel had to take her up to her room. Well, this morbid sensitiveness is most unhealthy. If I walk out on the terrace, she follows, thinking that I have made an appointment to meet you. Jealousy of me fills up her whole mind. I assure you that I am most seriously alarmed. Something occurs every day —trifles, no doubt; and in anybody else they would mean nothing, but in her they mean a great deal.'

'But what do you propose?'

'Unless you intend to marry her—forgive me for speaking so plain—there is only one thing to do. I must leave.'

'No, no; you must not leave! She could not live alone with me. But does she want you to leave?'

'No; that is the worst of it. I have proposed it; she will not hear of it; to mention the subject is to provoke a scene. She is afraid if I left that you would come and see me; and the very thought of my escaping her vigilance is intolerable.'

'It is very strange.'

'Yes, it is very strange; but, opposed though she be to all thoughts of it, I must leave.'

'As a favour I ask you to stay. Do me this service, I beg of you. I have set my heart on finishing my play this autumn. If it isn't finished now, it never will be finished; and your leaving would create so much trouble that all thought of work would be out of the question. Emily could not remain alone here with me. I should have to find another companion for her; and you know how difficult that would be. I'm worried quite enough as it is.' A look of pain passed through his eyes, and Mrs. Bentley wondered what he he could mean. 'No,' he said, taking her hands, 'we are good friends—are we not? Do me this service.

Stay with me until I finish this play ; then, if things do not mend, go, if you like, but not now. Will you promise me ? '

' I promise.'

' Thank you. I am deeply obliged to you.'

At the end of a long silence, Hubert said, ' Will you not come up-stairs, and let me read you the first act ? '

' I should like to, but I think it better not. If Emily heard that you had read me your play, she would not close her eyes to-night ; it would be tears and misery all the night through.'

XVI

THE study in which he had determined to write his masterpiece had been fitted up with taste and care. The floor was covered with a rare Persian carpet, and the walls were lined with graceful bookcases of Chippendale design; the volumes, half morocco, calf, and the yellow paper of French novels, showed through the diamond panes. The writing-table stood in front of the window; like the bookcases, it was Chippendale, and on the dark mahogany the handsome silver inkstand seemed to invite literary composition. There was a scent of flowers in the room. Emily had filled a bowl of old china with some pale September roses. The curtains were made of a modern cretonne—their colour was similar to the bowl of roses; and the large couch on which Hubert lay was covered with the same material. On one wall there was a sea-piece by Courbet, and upon another a river landscape, with rosy-tinted evening sky, by Corot. The chimney-piece was set out with a large gilt timepiece, and candelabra

in Dresden china. Hubert had bought these works of
art on the occasion of his last visit to London, about
two months ago.

It was twelve o'clock. He had finished reading his
second act, and the reading had been a bitter disappointment. The idea floated, pure and seductive, in
his mind; but when he tried to reduce it to a precise
shape upon paper, it seemed to escape in some vague,
mysterious way. Enticingly, like a butterfly it fluttered
before him; he followed like a child, eagerly—his brain
set on the mazy flight. It led him through a country
where all was promise of milk and honey. He followed,
sure that the alluring spirit would soon choose a flower;
then he would capture it. Often it seemed to settle.
He approached with palpitating heart; but lo! when
the net was withdrawn it was empty.

A look of pain and perplexity came upon his face;
he remembered the lodging at seven shillings a week in
the Tottenham Court Road. He had suffered there;
but it seemed to him that he was suffering more here.
He had changed his surroundings, but he had not
changed himself. Success and failure, despair and
hope, joy and sorrow, lie within and not without us.
His pain lay at his heart's root; he could not pluck
it forth, and its gratification seemed more than ever

impossible. He changed his position on the couch. Suddenly his thoughts said, 'Perhaps I am mistaken in the subject. Perhaps that is the reason. Perhaps there is no play to be extracted from it; perhaps it would be better to abandon it and choose another. For a few seconds he scanned the literary horizon of his mind. 'No, no!' he said bitterly, 'this is the play I was born to write. No other subject is possible; I can think of nothing else. This is all I can feel or see.' It was the second act that now defied his efforts. It had once seemed clear and of exquisite proportions; now no second act seemed possible: the subject did not seem to admit of a second act; and, clasping his forehead with his hands, he strove to think it out.

Any distraction from the haunting pain, now become chronic, is welcome, and he answers with a glad 'Come in!' the knock at the door.

'I'm sorry,' said Mrs. Bentley, 'for disturbing you, but I should like to know what fish you would like for your dinner—soles, turbot, or whiting? Immersed in literary problems as you are, I daresay these details are very prosaic; but I notice that later in the day——'

Hubert laughed. 'I find such details far more agreeable than literature. I can do nothing with my play.'

Aren't you getting on this morning?'

'No, not very well.'

'What do you think of turbot?'

'I think turbot very nice. Emily likes turbot.'

'Very well, then. I'll order turbot.'

As Mrs. Bentley was about to withdraw, she said, 'I'm sorry you are not getting on. What stops you now? That second act?'

'Come, you are not very busy. I'll read you the act as it stands, and then tell you how I think it ought to be altered. Nothing helps me so much as to talk it over; not only does it clear up my ideas, but it gives me desire to write. My best work has always been done in that way.'

'I really don't think I can stay. If Emily heard that you had been reading your play to me——'

'I'm tired of hearing of what Emily thinks. I can put up with a good deal, and I know that it is my duty to show much forbearance; but there is a limit to all things!' This was the first time Mrs. Bentley had seen him show either excitement or anger; she hardly knew him in this new aspect. In a moment the blonde calm of the Saxon had dropped from him, and some Celtic emphasis appeared in his speech. 'This hysterical girl,' he continued, 'is a sore burden. Tears

about this, and sighs about that; fainting fits because
I happen to take a chair next to yours. You may
depend upon it our lives are already the constant
gossip of the neighbourhood.'

'I know it is very annoying; and I, I assure you,
receive my share. Every look and word is misinterpreted. I must not stay here.'

'You must not go! I really want you. I assure
you that your opinion will be of value.'

'But think of Emily. It will make her wretched if she
hears of it. You do not know how it affects her. The
slightest thing! You hardly see anything; I see it all.'

'But there is no sense in it; it is pure madness.
I'm writing a play, trying to work out a most difficult
problem, and am in want of an audience, and I ask
you if you will be kind enough to let me read you the
act, and you cannot listen to it because—because—yes,
that's just it—because!'

'You do not know how she suffers. Let me go;
spare her the pain.'

'She is not the only one who suffers. Do you think
that I don't suffer? I've set my heart—my very life
is set on this play. I must get through with it; they
are all waiting for it. My enemies say I cannot write
it, but I shall if you will help me.'

"SOMETIMES, IN AN EXCITING PASSAGE, THE HANDS WERE CLASPED."

'Poor Emily's heart is equally broken. Her life is equally set——' Mrs. Bentley did not finish. Hubert just caught the words. Their significance struck him; he looked questioningly into Mrs. Bentley's eyes; then, pretending not to have understood, he begged her to remain. With the air of one who yields to a temptation, she came into the room. He felt strangely happy, and, drawing over an arm-chair for her, he threw himself on the couch. He noticed that she wore a loose white jacket, and once during the reading of the act he was conscious of a beautiful hand hanging over the rail of the chair. Sometimes, in an exciting passage, the hands were clasped. The black slippers and the slender black-stockinged ankles showed beneath the skirt; and when he raised his eyes from the manuscript, he saw the blonde face and hair, and the pale eyes were always fixed upon him. She listened with a keen and penetrating interest to his criticism of the act, agreeing with him generally, sometimes quietly contesting a point, and with some strange fascination drawing new and unexpected ideas from him; and in the intellectual warmth of her femininity his brain seemed to clear and his ideas took new shape.

'Ah,' he said, after two hours' delightful talk, 'how much I'm indebted to you! At last I see my mistakes; in two days I shall have written the act. And he wrote rapidly for nearly two hours, reconstructing the opening scenes of his second act.' He then threw himself on the couch, smoked a cigar, and after half an hour's rest continued writing till dinner-time.

When he came down-stairs, the thought of what he had been writing was still so vivid in him that he did not notice at once the silence of those with whom he was dining. He complimented Mrs. Bentley on the freshness of the turbot; she hardly answered; and then he became aware that something had gone wrong. What? Only one thing was possible. Emily had heard that Mrs. Bentley had been in his study. Looking from the woman to the girl, he saw that the latter had been weeping. She was still in a highly hysterical state, and might burst into tears and fly from the dinner-table at any moment. His face changed expression, and it was with difficulty that he restrained his temper. His life had been made up of a constant recurrence of these scenes, and he was wholly weary of them; and the thought of the absolute want of reason in the causeless jealousy, and the misery that these little bickerings made of his life, exasperated him beyond measure. The dinner proceeded in silence, and every slight remark was a presage of storm.

196

Hubert hoped the girl would say nothing until the servant left the room, and with that view he never spoke a word except to ask the ladies what they would take to eat. These tactics might have succeeded if Mrs. Bentley had not unfortunately said that next week she intended to go to London for a couple of days. 'The Eastwicks are there now, and they've asked me to stay with them.'

'I think I shall go up with you. I want to go to London,' said Emily.

'It will be very nice if you'll come; but we cannot both stay with the Eastwicks; they have only one spare room.'

'I suppose you'd like me to go to an hotel.'

'My dear Emily, how can you think of such a thing? A young girl like you could not stay at an hotel alone. I shall be only too pleased if you will go to the Eastwicks; I will go to the hotel.'

Emily's lip quivered, and in the irritating silence both Hubert and Mrs. Bentley saw that she was trying to overcome her passion. They fervently hoped she would succeed; for at that moment the servant was handing round the wine, and the time he took to accomplish this service seemed endless. He had filled the last glass, had handed round the dessert,

and was preparing to leave the room when Emily
said—

'The hotel will suit you very well. You'll be free
to see Hubert whenever you like.'

Hubert looked up quickly, hoping Mrs. Bentley
would not answer, but before he could make a sign she
said—

'What do you mean, Emily? I did not know that
Hubert was going to London.'

'You hardly expect me to believe that, do you?'

The servant was still in the room; but no look of
astonishment appeared on his face, and Hubert hoped
he had not heard. An awful silence glowered upon the
dinner-table. The moment the door closed Hubert
said, turning angrily to Emily—

'Really, I am quite surprised, Emily, that you should
make such observations in the presence of servants !
This has been going on quite long enough; you are
making the house intolerable. I shall not be able to
live here any longer.'

Emily burst into a passionate flood of tears. She
declared she was wretchedly miserable, and that she
fully understood that Hubert had begun to regret that
he had asked her to stay at Ashwood. Everything had
been taken from her; every one was against her. Her

sobs shook her frail little frame as if they would break it, and Hubert's heart was wrung at the sight of such genuine suffering.

'My dear Emily, I assure you you are mistaken. We both love you very much.' He got up from his chair, and, putting his arm about her, besought her to dry her eyes; but she shook him passionately from her, and fled from the room.

Three days after, Emily tore up one of her songs, because Mrs. Bentley had sung it without her leave. And so on and so on, week after week. No sooner was one quarrel allayed than signs of another began to appear. Hubert despaired. 'How is this to end?' he asked himself every day. Mrs. Bentley begged him to cancel her promise, and allow her to go. But that was impossible. He could not remain alone with Emily; if he left her she would not fail to believe that he had gone after her rival. The situation had become so tense that they ended by discussing these questions almost without reserve. To make matters worse, Emily had begun visibly to lose her health. There was neither colour in her cheeks nor light in her eyes; she hardly slept at all, and had grown more than ever like a little shadow. The doctor had been summoned, and, after prescribing a tonic, had advised quiet and avoidance of all excitement. Therefore Hubert and Mrs. Bentley agreed never to meet except when Emily was present, and then strove to speak as little as possible to each other. But the very fact of having to restrain themselves in looks, glances, and every slightest word—for Emily misinterpreted all things —whetted their appetites for each other's society.

In the misery of his study, when he watched the sheet of paper, he often sought relief in remembrance of her sweet manner, and the happy morning he had spent in her companionship. What he had written under the direct influence of her inspiration still seemed to him to be less bad than the rest of his play ; and he began to feel sure that, if ever this play were written, it would be written in the benign charm of her sweet encouragement, in the reposeful shadow of her presence. But that presence was forbidden him—that presence that seemed so necessary ; and for what reason ? Turning on the circumstances of his life, he raged against them, declaring that it would be folly to allow his very life's desire to be frittered away to gratify a young girl's caprice,—a caprice which in a few years she would laugh at. And whenever he was not thinking of his play, he remembered the charm of Mrs. Bentley's company, and the beneficent effect it had on his work. He had never known a woman he had liked so much, and he felt—he started at the thought, so like an inspiration did it seem to him—that the only possible solution of the present situation was his marriage with her. Once he was married, Emily would soon learn to forget him. They would take her up to London for the season; and, amid the healthy excitement of balls and parties, her girlish fancy would evaporate. No doubt she would meet again the young cavalry officer whose addresses she had received so coldly. She would be sure to meet him again—be sure to think him the most charming man in the world; they would marry, and she would make him the best possible wife. The kindest action they could do Emily would be to marry. There was nothing else to do, and they must do something, or else the girl would die. It seemed wonderful to Hubert that he had not thought of all this before. 'It is the very obvious solution of the problem,' he said; and his heart beat as he heard Mrs. Bentley's step in the corridor. It died away in the distance; but a few days after, when he heard it again, he jumped from his chair, and ran to the door. 'Come,' he said, 'I want to speak to you.'

'No, no, I beg of you!'

'I must speak to you!' He laid his hand upon her

arm, and said, 'I beg of you. I have something to say —it is of great importance. Come in.'

They looked at each other a moment, and it seemed as if they could see into each other's souls. Then a look of yielding passed into her eyes, and she said—

'Well, what is it?'

The familiarity of the words struck her, and she saw by the kindling tenderness in his eyes that they had given him pleasure. She almost knew he was going to tell her that he loved her. He looked towards the open door, and, guessing his intention, she said—

'Don't shut it! Speak quickly. Remember that she may pass at any moment. Were she to find us together, she would suffer; it would be tears and reproaches. What you have to say to me is about her?'

'Of course; we never speak of anything else. But we must not be overheard. I must shut the door.' She noticed a certain embarrassment in his manner. Suddenly relinquishing his intention to take her hands, he said—

'This cannot go on; our lives are being made unbearable. You agree with me—do you not?'

'Yes,' she said, with a curious inquiring look in her eyes. 'You had better let me leave. It is the only way out of the difficulty.'

'You know very well, Julia, that that is impossible.'

It was the first time he had used her Christian name, and she knew now he was going to ask her to marry him. A frightened look passed into her face; she turned from him; he took her hands.

'No, Julia,' he said; 'there is another and better way out of the difficulty. You will stop here—you will be my wife?' Reading the look of pain that had come into her eyes, he said, 'You will not refuse me? I want you—I can do nothing without you. If you leave me, I shall never be able to write my play; it can only be written under your influence. I love you, Julia!' She allowed him to draw her towards him, and then she broke away.

'Oh,' she said, 'why do you say these things? You only make my task harder. You know that I cannot betray my friend. Why do you tempt me to do a dishonourable action?'

'A dishonourable action! What do you mean? It is the only way to save her. Once we are married, she will forget. No doubt she will shed a few tears; but to save the body we must often lose a limb. It is even so. Things cannot go on as they are. We cannot watch her withering away under our very eyes; and that is what is actually happening. I have thought it all over, considered it from every point of view, and have come to the conclusion that—that, well, that we had better marry. You must have seen that I always liked you. I did not myself know how much until a few days ago. Say that I am not wholly disagreeable to you.'

'No; I will not listen to you! My conscience tells me plainly where my duty lies. Not for all the world will I play Emily false. I shudder to think of such a thing; it would be the basest ingratitude. I owe everything to her. When I hadn't a penny in the world, and when in my homelessness I wrote to Mr. Burnett, she pleaded in my favour, and decided him to take me as a companion. No, no! a thousand times no! Let go my hands. Do you not know what it is to be loyal?'

'I hope I do. But, as I have explained, it is the only solution. The romantic attachments of young girls, unless nipped in the bud, often end fatally. Do you not see how ill she is looking? She is wearing her life away. We shall be acting in her best interests. Besides, she is not the only person to be considered. Do I not love you? Are you not the very woman whose influence, whose guidance, is necessary, so that I should succeed? Without your help I shall never write my play. A woman's influence is neccssary to every undertaking. The greatest writers owe their best inspiration to——'

'Her heart is as closely set upon you as yours is upon your play.'

'But,' cried Hubert, 'I do not love her! Under no circumstances would I marry her. That I swear to you. If she and I were alone on a desert island——'

Julia looked at him one moment doubtingly, inquiringly. Then she said—

'Hers is no evanescent fancy, but a passion that goes to the very roots of her nature, and will kill her if it be not satisfied.'

'Or cut out in time.'

'I must leave.'

'That will not mend matters.'

'My departure will, at all events, remove all cause for jealousy; and when I am gone you may learn to love her.'

'No; that I swear is impossible!'

'You very likely think so now; but I'm bound to give her every chance of winning you.'

'I say again that that is impossible! I have never seen a woman except yourself I could marry. I tell you so: believe me as you like. . . . In this matter you are acting like a woman,—you allow your emotions and not your intellect to lead you. By acting thus, you are certainly sacrificing two lives—hers and mine. Of your own I do not speak, not knowing what is passing in your heart; but if by any chance you should care for me, you are adding your own happiness to the general holocaust.' Neither spoke again for some time.

'Why should you not marry her?' Julia said, at the end of a long silence. 'Some people think her quite a pretty girl.'

The lovers looked at each other and smiled sadly. And then, in pathetic phrases, Hubert tried to explain why he could never love Emily. He spoke of his age, and of difference of tastes,—he liked clever women. The conversation fell. At the end of a long silence, Julia said—

'There is nothing for it but my departure, and the sooner the better.'

'You are not in earnest? You are surely not in earnest?'

'Yes, indeed I am.'

'Then, if you go, you must take her with you. She cannot remain here alone with me. And even if she could, I could not live with her. Her folly has destroyed any liking I may have ever had for her. You 'll have to take her with you.'

'She would not come with me. I spoke to her once of a trip abroad.'

' And she refused ? '

'She said she only wanted things to go on just as they are.'

XVII

In some trepidation Julia knocked. Receiving no
reply, she opened the door, and her candle burnt in
what a moment before must have been inky darkness.
Emily lay on her bed—on the edge of it; and the
only movement she made was to avert her eyes
from the light. ' 'What! all alone in this darkness,
Emily ! . . . Shall I light your candles?' She had
to repeat the question before she could get an
answer.

'No, thank you; I want nothing; I have no wish to
see anything. I like the dark.'

' Have you been asleep?'

'No; I have not. . . . Why do you come to torment
me ? It cannot matter to you whether I lie in the dark
or the light. Oh, take that candle away ! it is blinding
me.' Julia put the candle on the washstand. Then
full of pity for the grieving girl, she stood, her hand
resting on the bed-rail.

' Aren't you coming down to dinner, Emily ? Come,

let me pour out some water for you. When you have bathed your eyes——'

'I don't want any dinner.'

'It will look very strange if you remain in your room the whole evening. You do not want to vex him, do you?'

'I suppose he is very angry with me. But I did not mean to vex him. Is he very angry?'

'No, he is not angry at all; he is merely distressed. You distress him dreadfully when——'

'I don't know why I should distress him. I'm sure I don't mean to. You know more about it than I. You are always whispering together—talking about me.'

'I assure you, Emily, you are mistaken. Mr. Price and I have no secrets whatever.'

'Why should you tell me these falsehoods? They make me so miserable.'

'Falsehoods, Emily! When did you ever know me to tell a falsehood?'

'You say you have no secrets! Do you think I am blind? You think, I suppose, I did not see you showing him a ring? You took it off, too; and I suppose you gave it to him,—an engagement ring, very likely.'

'I lost a stone from my ring, and I asked Mr. Price if he would take the ring to London and have the stone replaced. . . . That is all. So you see how your imagination has run away with you.'

Emily did not answer. At last she said, breaking the silence abruptly—

'Is he very angry? Has he gone to his study? Do you think he will come down to dinner?'

'I suppose he'll come down for dinner.'

'Will you go and ask him?'

'I hardly see how I can do that. He is very busy. . . . And if you would listen to any advice of mine, it would be to leave him to himself as much as possible for the present. He is so taken up with his play; I know he's most anxious about it.'

'Is he? I don't know. He never speaks to me about it. I hate that play, and I hate to see him go up to that study! I cannot understand why he should trouble himself about writing plays; he doesn't want the money, and it can't be agreeable sitting up there all alone thinking. . . . It is easy to see that it only makes him unhappy. But you encourage him to go on with it. Oh yes, you do; there's no use saying you don't. You are always talking to him about it; you bring the conversation up. You think I don't see how you do it, but I do; and you like doing it, because then you have him all to yourself. I can't talk to him about that play; and I wouldn't if I could, for it only makes him unhappy. But you don't care whether he's unhappy or not; you only think of yourself.'

'You surely don't believe what you are saying is true? To-morrow you will be sorry for what you have said. You cannot think that I would deceive you, Emily? Remember what friends we have been.'

'I remember everything. You think I don't; but I do. And you think also that there's no reason why I should be miserable; but there is. Because you do not feel my misery, you think it doesn't exist. I daresay you think, too, that you are very good and kind; but you aren't. You think you deceive me; but you don't. I know all that is passing between you and Hubert. I know a great deal more than I can explain. . . .'

'But tell me, Emily, what is it you suspect? What do you accuse me of?'

'I accuse you of nothing. Can't you understand that things may go wrong without it being any one's fault in particular?'

Julia wondered how Emily could think so wisely. She seemed to have grown wiser in her grief. But grief helped her no further in her instinctive perception of the truth, and she resumed her puerile attack on her friend.

'Nothing has gone well with me ever since you came here. I was disinherited; and I daresay you were glad, for you knew that if the money did not come to me it would go to Hubert, and I do know——'

'What are you saying, Emily? I never heard of such wild accusations before! You know very well that I never set eyes on Mr. Price until he came down here.'

'How should I know what you know or don't know? But I know that all my life every one has been plotting against me. And I cannot make out why. I never did harm to any one.'

The conversation paused. Emily flung herself back on the pillow. Not even a sob. The candle burned like a long yellow star in the shadows, yielding only sufficient light for Julia to see the outlines of a somewhat untidy room,—an old-fashioned mahogany wardrobe, cloudy and black, upon old-fashioned grey paper, some cardboard boxes, and a number of china ornaments, set out on a small table covered with a tablecloth in crewel-work.

'I would do anything in the world for you, Emily. I am your best friend, and yet——'

'I have no friend. I don't believe in friends. You think people are your friends, and then you find they are not.'

'How can I convince you of the injustice of your suspicions?'

'I see all plainly enough; it is fate, I suppose. . . . Selfishness. We all think of ourselves—we can't help it; and that's what makes life so miserable. . . . He would be a very good match. You have got him to like you. Perhaps you didn't intend to; but you have done it all the same.'

'But, Emily dear, listen! There is no question of marriage between me and Mr. Price. If you will only have patience, things will come right in the end.'

'For you, perhaps.'

'Emily, Emily! . . . You should try to understand things better.'

'I feel them, even if I don't understand.'

'Admit that you were wrong about the ring. Have I not convinced you that you were wrong?'

Emily did not answer. But at the end of a long silence, in which she had been pursuing a different train of thought, she said, 'Then you mean that he has never asked you to marry him?'

The directness of the question took Julia by surprise,

and, falsehood being unnatural to her, she hesitated, hardly knowing what to answer. Her hesitation was only momentary; but in that moment there came up such a wave of pity for the grief-stricken girl that she lied for pity's sake, 'No, he never asked me to marry him. I assure you that he never did. If you do not believe me——' As she was about to say, 'I will swear it if you like,' an irresponsible sensation of pride in her ownership of his love surged up through her, overwhelming her will, and she ended the sentence, 'I am very sorry, but I cannot help it.'

The words were still well enough; it was in the accent that the truth transpired. And then yielding still further to the force which had subjugated her will, she said—

. 'I admit that we have talked about a great many things.' (Again she strove not to speak, but the words rose red-hot to her lips.) 'He has said that he would like to marry, but I should not think of accepting——'

'Then it is just as I thought!' Emily cried; 'he wants to get rid of me!'

Julia was shocked and surprised at the depth of disgraceful vanity and cowardice which special circumstances had brought within her consciousness. The Julia Bentley of the last few moments was not the Julia

Bentley she was accustomed to meet and interrogate, and she asked herself how she might exorcise the meanness that had so unexpectedly appeared in her. Should she pile falsehood on falsehood? She felt it would be cruel not to do so; but Emily said, 'He wants to marry to get rid of me, and not because he loves you.' Then it was hard to deny herself the pleasure of telling the whole truth; but she mastered her desire of triumph, and, actuated by nothing but sincerest love and pity, she said—

'Oh, Emily dear, he never asked me to marry him; he does not love me at all! Why will you not believe me?'

'Because I cannot!' she cried passionately. 'I only ask to be left alone.'

'A little patience, Emily, and all will come right. Mr. Price does not want to get rid of you. You wrong him just as you wrong me. He has often said how much he likes you; indeed he has.' Although speaking from the bottom of her heart, it seemed to Julia that she was playing the part of a cruel, false woman, who was designingly plotting to betray a helpless girl; and not understanding why this was so, she was at once puzzled and confused. It seemed to her that she was being borne on in a wind of destiny, and her will seemed to beat vainly against it, like a bird's wings when a storm is blowing. She was conscious of a curious powerlessness; it surprised her, and she could not understand why she continued talking, so vain and useless did words seem to her—an idle patter. She continued—

'You think that I stand between you and Mr. Price. Now, I assure you that it is not so. I tell you I should refuse Mr. Price, even if he were to ask me to marry him, here, at this very moment. I pledge you my word on this. Give me your hand, Emily. You will not refuse it?' Emily gave her hand. 'It is quite ridiculous to promise, for he will never ask me; but I promise not to marry him even if he should ask me.' She gave the promise, determined to keep it; and yet she knew she would not keep it. She argued passionately with herself, a prey to an inward dread; for no matter how firmly she forced resolution upon resolution, they all seemed to melt in her soul like snow on a blazing fire. Then, determined to rid her-self of a numb sensation of powerlessness, and achieve the end she desired, she said, 'I'll tell you, Emily, what I'll do. I'll not stay here; I will go away. Let me go away, dear, and then it will be all right.'

'No, no! you mustn't leave; I don't want you to

leave. It would be said everywhere that I had you sent away. . . . You promise me not to leave?' Raising herself, Emily clung to Julia's arm, detaining her until she had extorted the desired promise.

'Very well; I promise,' she said sadly. 'But I think you are wrong; indeed I do. I have always thought that "the only solution of the problem" was my departure.' Memory had betrayed her into Hubert's own phrase.

'Why should you go? You think, 1 suppose, that I'm in love with Hubert? I'm not. All I want is for things to go on just the same—for us to be friends as we were before.'

'Very well, Emily—very well. . . . But in the meantime you must not neglect your meals as you have been doing lately. If you don't take care, you'll lose your health and your looks. I have been noticing how thin you are looking.'

'I suppose you have told him that I am looking thin and ill. . . . Men like tall, big, healthy women like you—don't they?'

'I see, Emily, that it is hopeless; every word one utters is misinterpreted. Dinner will be ready in a few minutes; or, if you like, I will dine up-stairs; and you and Mr. Price——'

'But is he coming down to dinner? I thought you said he had gone to his study; sometimes he dines there.'

'I can tell you nothing about Mr. Price. I don't know whether he'll dine up-stairs or down.'

At that moment a knock was heard at the door, and the servant announced that dinner was ready. 'Mr. Price has sent down word, ma'am, that he is very busy writing; he hopes you'll excuse him, and he'll be glad if you will send him his dinner up on a tray.'

'Very well; I shall be down directly.'

The slight interruption had sufficed to calm Julia's irritation, and she stood waiting for Emily. But seeing that she showed no signs of moving, she said, 'Aren't you coming down to dinner, Emily?' It was a sense of strict duty that impelled the question, for her heart sank at the prospect of spending the evening alone with the girl. But seeing the tears on Emily's cheeks, she sat down beside her, and said, 'Dearest Emily, if you would only confide in me!'

'There's nothing to confide. . . .'

'You mustn't give way like this; you really mustn't. Come down and have some dinner.'

'It is no use; I couldn't eat anything.'

'He may come into the drawing-room in the course of the evening, and will be so disappointed and grieved to hear that you have not been down.'

'No; he will spend the whole evening in his room; we shall not see him again.'

'But if I go and ask him to come; if I tell him——'

'No; do not speak to him about me; he'd only say that I was interfering with his work.'

'That is unjust, Emily; he has never reproached you with interfering with his work. Shall I go and tell him that you won't come down because you think he is angry with you?'

Ten minutes passed, and no answer could be obtained from Emily—only passionate and illusive refusals, denials, prayer to be left alone; and these mingled with irritating suggestions that Julia had better go at once, that Hubert might be waiting for her. But Julia bore patiently with her and did not leave her until Hubert sent to know why his dinner was delayed.

Emily had begun to undress; and, tearing off her things, she hardly took more than five minutes to get into bed.

'Shall I light a candle?' Julia asked before leaving.

'No, thank you.'

'Shall I send you up some soup?'

'No; I could not touch it.'

'You are not going to remain in the dark? Let me light a night-light?'

'No, thank you; I like the dark.'

XVIII

Hubert and Mrs. Bentley stood by the chimney-piece
in the drawing-room, waiting for the doctor; they had
left him with Emily, and stood facing each other absorbed in thought, when the door opened, and the
doctor entered.   Hubert said—

'What do you think, Doctor?   Is she seriously ill?'

'There is nothing, so far as I can make out, organic-
ally the matter with her, but the system is running
down.   She is very thin and weak.   I shall prescribe a
tonic, but——'

'But what, doctor?'

'She seems to be suffering from extreme depression
of spirits.   Do you know of any secret grief—any love
affair?   At her age, anything of that sort fills the entire
mind, and the consequences are often grave.'

'And supposing it were so, what would be your advice?   Change of air and scene?'

'Certainly.'

'Have you spoken to her on the subject?'

'Yes; but she says she will not leave Ashwood.'

'We cannot send her away by force. What would you advise us to do?'

'There's nothing to be done. We must hope for the best. There is no immediate cause for fear. . . . But, by the way, she looks as if she suffered from sleeplessness.'

'Yes, she does; but she has been ordered chloral. Any harm in that?'

'In her case, it is a necessity; but do you think she takes it?'

'Oh yes, she has been taking choral.'

The conversation paused; the doctor went over to the writing-table, wrote a prescription, made a few remarks, and took his leave, announcing his intention of returning that day fortnight.

Hubert said, and his tone implied reference to some anterior conversation, 'We are powerless in this matter. You see we can do nothing. We only succeed in making ourselves unhappy; we do not change in anything. I am wretchedly unhappy!'

'Believe me,' she said, raising her arms in a beautiful feminine movement, 'I do not wish to make you unhappy.'

'Then why do you persist? Why do you refuse

to take the only step that may lead us out of this difficulty?'

'How can you ask me? Oh, Hubert, I did not think you could be so cruel! It would be a shameful action.'

It was the first time she had used his Christian name, and his face changed expression.

'I cannot,' she said, 'and I will not, and I do not understand how you can ask me—you who are so loyal, how can you ask me to be disloyal?'

'Spare me your reproaches. Fate has been cruel. I have never told you the story of my life. I have suffered deeply; my pride has been humiliated, and I have endured hunger and cold; but those sufferings were light compared to this last misfortune.'

She looked at him with sublime pity in her eyes. 'I do not conceal from you,' she said, 'that I love you very much. I, too, have suffered, and I had thought for one moment that fate had vouchsafed me happiness; but, as you would say—the irony of life.'

'Julia, do not say you never will?'

'We cannot look into the future. But this I can say—I will not do Emily any wrong, and so far as is in my power I will avoid giving her pain. There is only one way out of this difficulty. I must leave this house as soon as I can persuade her to let me go.'

The door opened; involuntarily the speakers moved apart; and though their faces and attitudes were strictly composed when Emily entered, she knew they had been standing closer together.

'I'm afraid I'm interrupting you,' she said.

'No, Emily; pray do not go away. We were only talking about you.'

'If I were to leave every time you begin to talk about me, I should spend my life in my room. I daresay you have many faults to find. Let me hear all about your fresh discoveries.'

It was a thin November day: leaves were whirling on the lawn, and at that moment one blew rustling down the window-pane. And, even as it, she seemed a passing thing. Her face was like a plate of fine white porcelain, and the deep eyes filled it with a strange and magnetic pathos; the abundant chestnut hair hung in the precarious support of a thin tortoiseshell; and there was something unforgetable in the manner in which her aversion for the elder woman betrayed itself—a mere nothing, and yet more impressive than any more obvious and therefore more vulgar expression of dislike would have been.

'A little patience, Emily. You will not have me here much longer.'

'I suppose that I am so disagreeable that you cannot live with me. Why should you go away?'

'My dear Emily, you must not excite yourself. The doctor——'

'I want to know why she said she was going to leave. Has she been complaining about me to you? What is her reason for wanting to go?'

'We do not get on together as we used to—that is all, Emily. I can please you no longer.'

'It is not my fault if we do not get on. I don't see why we shouldn't, and I do not want you to go.'

'Emily, dear, everything shall be as you like it.'

The girl looked at him with the shy, doubting look of an animal that would like, and still does not dare, to go to the beckoning hand. How frail seemed the body in the black dress! and how thin the arms in the black sleeves! Hubert took the little hand in his. At his touch a look of content and rest passed into her eyes, and she yielded herself as the leaf yields to the wind. She was all his when he chose. Mrs. Bentley left the room; and, seeing her go, a light of sudden joy illuminated the thin, pale face; and when the door closed, and she was alone with him, the bleak, un-happy look, which had lately grown strangely habitual to her, faded out of her face and eyes. He fetched her shawl, and took her hand again in his, knowing that by so doing he made her happy. He could not refuse her the peace from pain that these attentions brought her, though he would have held himself aloof from all women but one. She knew the truth well enough; but they who suffer much think only of the cessation of pain. He wondered at the inveigling content that introduced itself into her voice, face, and gesture. Settling herself comfortably on the sofa, she said—

'Now tell me what the doctor said. Did he say I would soon recover? Did he say that I was very bad? Tell me all.'

'He said that you ought to have a change—that you should go south somewhere.'

'And you agree with him that I ought to go away?'

'Is he not the best judge?—the doctor's orders!'

'Then you, too, have learnt to hate me. You, too, want to send me away?'

'My dear Emily, I only want to do as you like. You asked me what the doctor said, and I told you.'

Hubert got up and walked aside. He passed his hand across his eyes. He could hardly contain himself; the emotion that discussion with this sick girl caused him went to his head. She looked at him curiously, watching his movement, and he failed to understand what pleasure it could give her to have him by her side, knowing, as she clearly did, that his heart was elsewhere. Turning suddenly, he said—

'But tell me, Emily, how are you feeling? You are, after all, the best judge.'

'I feel rather weak. I should get strong enough if——'

She paused, as if waiting for Hubert to ask her to finish the sentence. But he hurriedly turned the conversation.

'The doctor said you looked as if you had not had any sleep for several nights. I told him that that was strange, for you were taking chloral.'

'I sleep well enough,' she said. 'But sometimes life seems so sad, that I do not think I shall be able to bear with it any longer. You do not know how unfortunate I have been. When I was a child, father and mother used to quarrel always, and I was the only child. That was why Mr. Burnett asked me to come and live at Ashwood. I came at first on a visit; and when father and mother died, he said he wished to adopt me. I thought he loved me; but his love was only selfishness. No one has ever loved me. I feel so utterly alone in this world—that is why I am unhappy.'

Her eyes filled with tears, and at the sight of her tears Hubert's feelings were overwrought, and again he had to walk aside. He would give her all things; but she was dying for him, and he could not save her. No longer was there any disguisement between them. The words they uttered were as nothing, so clearly did the thought shine out of their eyes, 'I am dying of love for you,' and then the answer, 'I know that is so, and I cannot help it.' Her whole soul was spoken in her eyes, and he felt that his eyes betrayed him equally plainly. They stood in a sort of mental nakedness. The woman no longer sought for words to cover herself with; the man did, but he did not find them. They had not spoken for some time; they had been thinking of each other. At last she said, and with the querulous perversity of the sick—

'But even if I wished to go abroad, with whom could I go?'

Hubert fell into the trap, and, noticing the sudden brightness in his eyes, a cloud of disappointment shadowed hers. 'Of course, with Mrs. Bentley. I assure you, my dear Emily, that you——'

'No, no, I am not mistaken! She hates me, and I cannot bear her. It is she who is making me ill.'

'Hate you! Why should she hate you?'

Emily did not reply. Hubert watched her, noticing the pallor of her cheek, so entirely white and blue, hardly a touch of warm colour anywhere, even in the shadow of the heavy hair.

'I would give anything to see you friends again.'

'That is impossible! I can never be friends with Julia as I once was. She has—— No, never can we be friends again. But why do you always take her part against me? That is what grieves me most. If only you thought—— '

'Emily dear, these are but idle fancies. You are mistaken.'

The conversation fell. The girl lay quite still, her hands clasped across the shawl, her little foot stretched beyond the limp black dress, the hem of which fell over the edge of the grey sofa. Hubert sat by her on a low chair, and he looked into the fire, whose light wavered over the walls, now and again bringing the face of one of the pictures out of the darkness. The wind whined about the windows. Then, speaking as if out of a dream, Emily said—

'Julia and I can never be friends again — that is impossible.'

'But what has she done?' Hubert asked incautiously, regretting his words as soon as he had uttered them.

'What has she done?' she said, looking at him curiously. 'Well, one thing, she has got it reported that—that I am in love with you, and that that is the reason of my illness.'

'I am sure she never said any such thing. You are entirely mistaken. Mrs. Bentley is incapable of such wickedness.'

'A woman, when she is jealous, will say anything. If she did not say it, can you tell me how it got about?'

'I don't believe any one ever said such a thing.'

'Oh yes, lots have said so—things come back to me. Julia always was jealous of me. She cannot bear me to speak to you. Have you not noticed how she follows us? Do you think she would have left the room just now if she could have helped it?'

'If you think this is so, had she not better leave?'

Emily did not answer at once. Motionless she lay on the sofa, looking at the grey November day with vague eyes that bespoke an obsession of hallucination.

Suddenly she said, 'I do not want her to go away. She would spread a report that I was jealous of her, and had asked you to send her away. No; it would not be wise to send her away. Besides,' she said, fixing her eyes, now full of melancholy reproach, 'you would like her to remain.'

'I have said before, Emily, and I assure you I am speaking the truth, I want you to do what you like. Say what you wish to be done, and it shall be done.'

'Is that really true? I thought no one cared for me. You must care for me a little to speak like that.'

'Of course I care for you, Emily.'

'I sometimes think you might have if it had not been for that play; for, of course, I'm not clever, and cannot discuss it with you. . . . Julia, I suppose, can—that is the reason why you like her. Am I not right?'

'Mrs. Bentley is a clever woman, who has read a great deal, and I like to talk an act over with her before I write it.'

'Is that all? Then why do people say you are going to marry her?'

'But nobody ever said so.'

'Oh yes, they have. Is it true?'

'No, Emily; it is not true.'

'Are you quite sure?'

'Yes, quite sure.'

'If that is so,' she said, turning her eyes on Hubert, and looking as if she could see right down into his soul, 'I shall get well very soon. Then we can go on just the same; but if you married her, I——'

'I what?'

'Nothing! I feel quite happy now. I did not want you to marry her. I could not bear it. It would be like having a step-mother—worse, for she would not have me here at all; she would drive me away.'

Hubert shook his head.

'You don't know Julia as well as I do. However, it is no use discussing what is not going to be. You have been very nice to-day. If you would be always nice, as you are to-day, I should soon get well.'

Her pale profile seemed very sharp in the fading twilight, and her delicate arms and thin bosom were full of the charm and fascination of deciduous things. She turned her face and looked at Hubert. 'You have made me very happy. I am content.'

He was afraid to look back at her, lest she should, in her subtle, wilful manner, read the thought that was passing in his soul. Even now she seemed to read it. She seemed conscious of his pity for her. So little would give her happiness, and that little was impossible. His heart was irreparably another's. But though Emily's eyes seemed to know all, they seemed to say, 'What matter? I regret nothing, only let things remain as they are.' And then her voice said—

'I think I could sleep a little; happiness has brought me sleep. Don't go away. I shall not be asleep long.' She looked at him, and dozed, and then fell asleep. Hubert waited till her breathing grew deeper; then he laid the hand he held in his by her side, and stole on tiptoe from the room.

The strain of the interview had become too intense; the house was unbearable. He went into the air. The November sky was drawing into wintry night; the grey clouds darkened, clinging round the long plain, overshadowing it, blotting out colour, leaving nothing but the severe green of the park, and the yellow whirling of dishevelled woods.

'I must,' he said to himself, 'think no more about it. I shall go mad if I do. Nature will find her own solution. God grant that it may be a merciful one! I can do nothing.' And to escape from useless consideration, to release his overwrought brain, he hastened his steps, extending his walk through the farthest woods. As he approached the lodge gate he came upon

Mrs. Bentley. She stood, her back turned from him, leaning on the gate, her thoughts lost in the long darkness of autumnal fields and woods.

'Julia!'

'You have left Emily. How did you leave her?'

'She is fast asleep on the sofa. She fell asleep. Then why should I remain? The house was unbearable. She went to sleep, saying she felt very happy.'

'Really! What induced such a change in her? Did you——'

'No; I did not ask her to marry me; but I was able to tell her that I was not going to marry you, and that seemed entirely to satisfy her.'

'Did she ask you?'

'Yes. And when I told her I was not, she said that that was all she wanted to know—that she would soon get well now. How we human beings thrive in each other's unhappiness!'

'Quite true, and we have been reproaching ourselves for our selfishness.'

'Yes, and hers is infinitely greater. She is quite satisfied not to be happy herself, so long as she can make sure of our unhappiness. And what is so strange is her utter unconsciousness of her own fantastic and hardly conceivable selfishness. . . . It is astonishing!'

'She is very young, and the young are naturally egotistic.'

'Possibly. Still, it is hardly more agreeable to encounter. Come, let's go for a walk ; and, above all things, let's talk no more about Emily.'

The roads were greasy, and the hedges were torn and worn with incipient winter, and when they dipped the town appeared, a reddish-brown mass in the blue landscape. Hubert thought of his play and his love ; but not separately—they seemed to him now as one indissoluble, indivisible thing ; and he told her that he never would be able to write it without her assistance. That she might be of use to him in his work was singularly sweet to hear, and the thought reached to the end of her heart, causing her to smile sadly, and argue vainly, and him to reply querulously. They walked for about a mile ; and then, wearied with sad expostulation, the conversation fell, and at the end of a long silence Julia said—

'I think we had better turn back.'

The suggestion filled Hubert's heart with rushing pain, and he answered—

'Why should we return ? I cannot go back to that girl. Oh, the miserable life we are leading !'

'What can we do ? We must go back ; we cannot

235

live in a tent by the wayside. We have no tent to set up.'

'Come to London, and be my wife.'

'No,' she said; 'that is impossible. Let us not speak of it.'

Hubert did not answer; and, turning their faces homeward, they walked some way in silence. Suddenly Hubert said—

'No; it is impossible. I cannot return. There is no use. I'm at the end of my tether. I cannot.'

She looked at him in alarm.

'Hubert,' she said, 'this is folly! I cannot return without you.'

'You ruin my life; you refuse me the only happiness. I'm more wretched than I can tell you!'

'And I! Do you think that I'm not wretched?' She raised her face to his; her eyes were full of tears. He caught her in his arms, and kissed her. The warm touch of her lips, the scent of her face and hair, banished all but desire of her.

'You must come with me, Julia. I shall go mad if you don't. I can care for no one but you. All my life is in you now. You know I cannot love that girl, and we cannot continue in this wretched life. There is no sense in it; it is a voluntary, senseless martyrdom!'

236

'Hubert, do not tempt me to be disloyal to my friend. It is cruel of you, for you know I love you. But no, nothing shall tempt me. How can I? We do not know what might happen. The shock might kill her. She might do away with herself.'

'You must come with me,' said Hubert, now completely lost in his passion. 'Nothing will happen. Girls do not do away with themselves; girls do not die of broken hearts. Nothing happens in these days. A few more tears will be shed, and she will soon become reconciled to what cannot be altered. A year or so after, we will marry her to a nice young man, and she will settle down a quiet mother of children.'

'Perhaps you are right.'

An empty fly, returning to the town, passed them. The fly-man raised his whip.

'Take you to the railway station in ten minutes!'

Hubert spoke quietly; nevertheless there was a strange nervousness in his eyes when he said—

'Fate comes to help me.; she offers us the means of escape. You will not refuse, Julia?'

Her upraised face was full of doubt and pain, and she was perplexed by the fly-man's dull eyes, his starved horse, his ramshackle vehicle, the wet road, the leaden sky. It was one of those moments when the familiar appears strange and grotesque. Then, gathering all her resolution, she said—

' No, no; it is impossible! Come back, come back.'

He caught her arm : quietly and firmly he led her across the road. ' You must listen to me. . . . We are about to take a decisive step. Are you sure that——'

' No, no, Hubert, I cannot; let us return home.'

' I go back to Ashwood! If I did, I should commit suicide.'

' Don't speak like that. . . . Where will you go ? '

' I shall travel. . . . I shall visit Italy and Greece. . . . I shall live abroad.'

' You are not serious ? '

' Yes, I am, Julia. That cab may not take both, but it certainly will take one of us away from Ashwood, and for ever.'

' Take you to Southwater, sir—take you to the station in ten minutes,' said the fly-man, pulling in his horse. A zig-zag fugitive thought passed : why did the fly-man speak of taking them to the station ? How was it that he knew where they wanted to go ? They stopped and wondered. The poor horse's bones stood out in strange projections, the round-shouldered little

fly-man sat grinning on his box, showing three long
yellow fangs. The vehicle, the horse, and the man, his
arm raised in questioning gesture, appeared in strange
silhouette upon the grey clouds, assuming portentous
aspect in their tremulous and excited imaginations.
'Take you to Southwater in ten minutes!' The voice
of the fly-man sounded hard, grating, and derisive in
their ears.

He had stopped in the middle of the road, and they
walked slowly past, through a great puddle, which
drenched their feet.

'Get in, Julia. Shall I open the door?'

'No, no; think of Emily. I cannot, Hubert,—I
cannot; it would kill her.'

The conversation paused, and in a long silence they
wondered if the fly-man had heard. Then they walked
several yards listening to the tramp of the hoofs, and
then they heard the fly-man strike his horse with the
whip. The animal shuffled into a sort of trot, and
as the carriage passed them the fly-man again raised
his arm and again repeated the same phrase, 'Drive
you to the station in ten minutes!' The carriage was
her temptation, and Julia hoped the man would linger
no longer. For the promise she had given to Emily lay
like a red-hot coal upon her heart; its fumes rose to

her head, and there were times when she thought they
would choke her, and she grew so sick with the pain
of self-denial that she could have thrown herself down
in the wet grass on the roadside, and laid her face on the
cold earth for relief. Would nothing happen? What
madness! Night was coming on, and still they followed
the road to Southwater. Rain fell in heavy drops.

'We shall get wet,' she murmured, as if she were
answering the fly-man, who had said again, 'Drive you
to the station in ten minutes!' She hated the man
for his persistency.

'Say you will come with me!' Hubert whispered;
and all the while the rain came down heavier.

'No, no, Hubert. . . . I cannot; I promised Emily
that I never would. I am going back.'

'Then we must say good-bye. I will not go back.'

'You don't mean it. You don't really intend me
to go back to Emily and tell her? . . . She will not
believe me; she will think I have sent you away to
gain my own end. Hubert, you mustn't leave me . . .
and in all this wet. See how it rains! I shall never
be able to get home alone.'

'I will drive you on as far as the lodge-gate; farther
than the lodge I will not go. Nothing in the world
shall tempt me to pass it.'

At a sign from Hubert the little fly-man scrambled down from his box. He was a little old man, almost hunchbacked, with small mud-coloured eyes and a fringe of white beard about his sallow, discoloured face. He was dressed in a pale yellow jacket and waistcoat, and they both noticed that his crooked little legs were covered with a pair of pepper-and-salt trousers. They felt sure he must have overheard a large part of their conversation, for as he opened the carriage door he grinned, showing his three yellow fangs. . . . His appearance was not encouraging. Julia wished he were different, and then she looked at Hubert. She longed to throw herself into his arms and weep. But at that moment the heavens seemed to open, and the rain came down like a torrent, thick and fast, splashing all along the road in a million splashes.

'Horrible weather, sir; shan't be long a-takin' you to Southwater. What part of the town be yer going to—the railway station?'

Julia still hesitated. The rain beat on their faces, and when some chilling drops rolled down her neck she instinctively sought shelter in the carriage.

'Drive me to the station as fast as you can. Catch the half-past five to London, and I'll give you five shillings.'

The leather thong sounded on the starved animal's hide, the crazy vehicle rocked from side to side, and the wet country almost disappeared in the darkness. Hedges and fields swept past them in faintest outline, here and there a blurred mass, which they recognised as a farm building. His arm was about her, and she heard him murmur over and over again—

'Dearest Julia, you are what I love best in the world.'

The words thrilled her a little, but all the while she saw Emily's eyes and heard her voice.

Hubert, however, was full of happiness—the sweet happiness of the quiet, docile creature that has at last obtained what it loves.

XIX

EMILY awoke shivering; the fire had gone out, the room was in darkness, and the house seemed strange and lonely. She rang the bell, and asked the servant if he had seen Mr. Price. Mr. Price had gone out late in the afternoon, and had not come in. Where was Mrs. Bentley? Mrs. Bentley had gone out earlier in the afternoon, and had not come in.

She suspected the truth at once. They had gone to London to be married. The servant lighted a candle, made up the fire, and asked if she would wait dinner. Emily made no answer, but sat still, her eyes fixed, looking into space. The man lingered at the door. At that moment her little dog bounded into the room, and, in a paroxysm of delight, jumped on his mistress's lap. She took him in her arms and kissed him, and this somewhat reassured the alarmed servant, who then thought it was no more than one of Miss Emily's queer ways. Dandy licked his mistress's face, and rubbed his rough head against her shoulder. He seemed more than usually affectionate that evening. Suddenly she caught him up in her arms, and kissed him passionately. 'Not even for your sake, dearest Dandy, can I bear with it any longer! We are all very selfish, and it is selfish of me to leave you, but I cannot help it.' Then a doubt crossed her mind, and she raised her head and listened to it. It seemed difficult to believe that he had told her a falsehood— a cruel, wicked falsehood—he who had been so kind. And yet—— Ah! yes, she knew well enough that it was all true; something told her so. The lancinating pain of doubt passed away, and she remained thinking of the impossibility of bearing any longer with the life.

An hour passed, and the servant came with the news that Mr. Price and Mrs. Bentley had gone to London; they had taken the half-past five train. 'Yes,' she said, 'I know they have.' Her voice was calm. There was a strange hollow ring in it, and the servant wondered. A few minutes after, dinner was announced; and to escape observation and comment she went into the dining-room, tasted the soup, and took a slice of mutton on her plate. She could not eat it. She gave it to Dandy. It was the last time she should feed him. How hungry he was! She hoped he would not care to eat it; he would not if he knew she was going to leave him.

In the drawing-room he insisted on being nursed; and alone, amid the faded furniture, watched over by the old portraits, her pale face fixed and her pale hands clasping her beloved dog, she sat thinking, brooding over the unhappiness, the incurable unhappiness, of her little life. She was absorbed in self, and did not rail against Hubert, or even Julia. Their personalities had somehow dropped out of her mind, and merely represented forces against which she found herself unable any longer to contend. Nor was she surprised at what had happened. There had always been in her some prescience of her fate. She and unhappiness had always seemed so inseparable, that she had never found it difficult to believe that this last misfortune would befall her. She had thought it over, and had decided that it would be unendurable to live any longer, and had borne many a terrible insomnia so that she might collect sufficient chloral to take her out of her misery; and now, as she sat thinking, she remembered that she had never, never been happy. Oh! the miserable evenings she used to spend, when a child, between her father and mother, who could not agree—why, she never understood. But she used to have to listen to her mother addressing insulting speeches to her father in a calm, even voice that nothing could alter; and, though both were dead and years divided her from that time, the memory survived, and she could see it all again—that room, the very paper on the wall, and her father being gradually worked up into a frenzy.

When she was left an orphan, Mr. Burnett had adopted her, and she remembered the joy of coming to Ashwood. She had thought to find happiness there; but there, as at home, fate had gone against her, and she was hardly eighteen when Mr. Burnett had asked her to marry him. She had loved that old man, but he had not loved her; for when she had refused to marry him he had broken all his promises and left her penniless, careless of what might become of her. Then she had given her whole heart to Julia, and Julia, too, had deceived her. And had she not loved Hubert?—no one would ever know how much; she did not know herself,—and had he not lied to her? Oh, it was very cruel to deceive a poor little girl in this heartless way! There was no heart in the world, that was it—and she was all heart; and her heart had been trampled on ever since she could remember. And when they came back they would revenge themselves upon her—insult her with their happiness; perhaps insist on sending her away.

Dandy drowsed on her lap. The servant brought in the tea, and when he returned to the kitchen he said he had never seen any one look so ghost-like as Miss Emily. The clock ticked loudly in the silence of the old room, the hands moving slowly towards ten. She waited for the hour to strike; it was then that she usually went to bed. Her thoughts moved as in a nightmare; and paramount in this chaotic mass of sensation was an acute sense of the deception that had been practised on her; with the consciousness, now firm and unalterable, that it had become impossible for her to live. When the clock struck she got up from her chair, and the movement seemed to react on her brain; her thoughts unclouded, and she went up-stairs thinking clearly of her love of this old house. The old gentleman in the red coat, his hand on his sword, looked on her benignly; and the lady playing the spinet smiled as sweetly as was her wont. Emily held up the candle to the picture of the windmill. She had always loved that picture, and the sad thought came that she should never see it again. Dandy, who had galloped up-stairs, stood looking through the banisters, wagging his tail.

The moment she got into her room she wrote the following note: 'I have taken an overdose of chloral. My life was too miserable to be borne any longer. I forgive those who have caused my unhappiness, and I hope they will forgive me any unhappiness I have caused them.' They were nothing to her now; they were beyond her hate, and the only pang she felt was parting with her beloved Dandy. There he stood looking at her, standing on the edge of the bed, waiting for her to cover him up and put him to sleep in his own corner. 'Yes, Dandy, in a moment, dear—have patience.' She looked round the little room, and, remembering all that she had suffered there, thought that the walls must be saturated with grief, like a sponge.

It was a common thing at that time for her to stand before the glass and address such words as these to herself: 'My poor girl, how I pity you, how I pity you!' And now, looking at herself very sadly, she said, 'My poor girl, I shall never pity you any more!' Having hung up her dress, she fetched a chair and took various doses of chloral out of the hollow top of her wardrobe, where she had hidden things all her life—sweets, novels, fireworks. They more than half-filled the tumbler; and, looking at the sticky, white liquid, she thought with repugnance of drinking so much of it. But, wanting to make quite sure of death, she resolved to take it all, and she undressed quickly. She was very cold when she got into bed. Then a thought struck her, and she got out of bed to add a postscript to her letter. 'I have only one request to make. I hope Dandy will always be taken care of.' Surprised that she had not wrapped him up and told him he was to go to sleep, the dog stood on the edge of the bed, watching her so earnestly that she wondered if he knew what she was going to do. 'No, you don't know, dear—do you? If you did, you wouldn't let me do it; you'd bark the house down, I know you would, my own darling.' Clasping him to her breast, she smothered him with kisses, then put him away in his corner, covering him over for the night.

She felt neither grief nor fear. Through much suffering, thought and sensation were, to a great extent, dead in her; and, in a sort of emotive numbness, she laid her candlestick in its usual place on the chair by her bedside; and, sitting up in bed, her night-dress carefully buttoned, holding the tumbler half-filled with chloral, she tried to take a dispassionate survey of her life. She thought of what she had endured, and what she would have to endure if she did not take it. Then she felt she must go, and without hesitation drank off the chloral. She placed the tumbler by the candlestick, and lay down, remembering vaguely that a long time ago she had decided that suicide was not wrong in itself. The last thing she remembered was the clock striking eleven.

For half an hour she slept like stone. Then her eyes opened, and they told of sickness now in motion within her. And, strangely enough, through the overpowering nausea rising from her stomach to her brain, the thought that she was not going to die appeared perfectly clear, and with it a sense of disappointment; she would have to begin it all over again. It was with great difficulty that she struck a match and lighted a candle. It seemed impossible to get up. At last she managed to slip her legs out of bed, and found she could stand, and through the various assaults of retching she thought of the letter: it must be destroyed; and, leaning in the corner against the wall and the wardrobe, she tried to recover herself. A dull, deep sleep was pressing on her brain, and she thought she would never be able to cross the room to where the letter was. Dandy looked out of his rug; she caught sight of his bright eyes.

'On cold and shaky feet she attempted to make her way towards the letter; but the room heaved up at her, and, fearing she should fall, and knowing if she did that she would not be able to regain her feet, she clung to the toilette-table. She must destroy that letter: if it were found, they would watch her; and, however impossible her life might become, she would not be able to escape from it. This consideration gave her strength for a final effort. She tore the letter into very small pieces, and then, clinging to a chair, strove to grasp the rail of the bed; but the bed rolled worse than any ship. Making a supreme effort, she got in; and then, neither dreams nor waking thoughts, but oblivion complete. Hours and hours passed, and when she opened her eyes her maid stood over the bed, looking at her.

'Oh, miss, you looked so tired and ill that I didn't wake you. You do seem poorly, miss. It is nearly two o'clock. Should you like to sleep a little longer, or shall I bring you up some breakfast?'

'No, no, no, thank you. I couldn't touch anything. I'm feeling wretched; but I'll get up.'

The maid tried to dissuade her; but Emily got out of bed, and allowed herself to be dressed. She was very weak—so weak that she could hardly stand up at the washstand; and the maid had to sponge her face and neck. But when she had drunk a cup of tea and eaten a little piece of toast, she said she felt better, and was able to walk into the drawing-room. She thought no more of death, nor of her troubles; thought drowsed in her; and in a passive, torpid state she sat looking into the fire till dinner-time, hardly caring to bestow a casual caress on Dandy, who seemed conscious of his mistress's neglect, for, in his sly, coaxing way, he sometimes came and rubbed himself against her feet. She went into the dining-room, and the servant was glad to see that she finished her soup, and, though she hardly tasted it, she finished a wing of a chicken, and also the glass of wine which the man pressed upon her. Half an hour after, when he brought out the tea, he found her sitting on her habitual chair nursing her dog, and staring into the fire so drearily that her look frightened him, and he hesitated before he gave her the letter which had just come up from the town; but it was marked 'Immediate.'

When he left the room she opened it. It was from Mrs. Bentley :—

'DEAREST EMILY,—I know that Hubert told you that he was not going to marry me. He thought he was not, for I had refused to marry him ; but a short time after we met in the park quite accidentally, and—well, fate took the matter out of our hands, and we are to be married to-morrow. Hubert insists on going to Italy, and I believe we shall remain there two months. We have made arrangements for your aunt to live with you until we come back ; and when we do come back, I hope all the little unpleasantnesses which have marred our friendship for this last month or two will be forgotten. So far as I am concerned, nothing shall be left undone to make you happy. Your will shall be law at Ashwood so long as I am there. If you would like to join us in Italy, you have only to say the word. We shall be delighted to have you.'

Emily could read no more. 'Join them in Italy !' She dashed the letter into the fire, and an intense hatred of them both pierced her heart and brain. It was the kiss of Judas. Oh, those hateful, lying words ! To live here with her aunt until they came back, to wait here quietly until she returned in triumph with him—him who had been all the world to her. Oh no ; that was not possible. Death, death—escape she must. But how? She had no more chloral. Suddenly she thought of the lake. 'Yes, yes ; the lake, the lake !' And then a keen, swift, passionate longing for death, such as she had not felt at all the night before, came upon her. There was the knowledge too that by killing herself she would revenge herself on those who had killed her. She was just conscious that her suicide would have this effect, but hardly a trace of such intention appeared in the letter she wrote; it was as melancholy and as brief as the letter she had torn up, and ended, like it, with a request that Dandy should be well looked after. She had only just directed the envelope when she heard the servant coming to take away the tea-things. She concealed the letter; and when his steps died away in the corridor and the house-door closed, she knew she could slip out unobserved. Instinctively she thought of her hat and jacket, and, without a shudder, remembered she would not need them. She sped down the pathway through the shadow of the firs.

It was one of those warm nights of winter when a sulphur-coloured sky hangs like a blanket behind the wet, dishevelled woods; and, though there was neither moon nor star, the night was strangely clear, and the shadow of the bridge was distinct in the water. When she approached the brink the swans moved slowly away. They reminded her of the cold; but the black obsession of death was upon her; and, hastening her steps, she threw herself forward. She fell into shallow water and regained her feet, and for a moment it seemed uncertain if she would wade to the bank or fling herself into a deeper place. Suddenly she sank, the water rising to her shoulders. She was lifted off her feet. A faint struggle, a faint cry, and then nothing—nothing but the whiteness of the swans moving through the sultry night slowly towards the island.

XX

ITS rich, inanimate air proclaimed the room to be an expensive bedroom in a first-class London hotel. Interest in the newly-married couple, who were to occupy the room, prompted the servants to see that nothing was forgotten; and as they lingered steps were heard in the passage, and Hubert and Julia entered. The maid-servants stood aside to let them pass, and one inquired if madame wanted anything, so that her eyes might be gratified with a last inquisition of the happy pair.

'How wonderful! oh, how wonderful! I don't think I ever saw any one act before like that—did you?'·

'She certainly had three or four moments that could not be surpassed. Her entrance in the sleep-walking scene—what vague horror! what pale presentiment! how she filled the stage! nothing seemed to exist but she.'

'And Ford; what did you think of Ford's Macbeth?'

'Very good. Everything he does is good. Talent; but the other has genius.'

'I shall never forget this evening. What an awful tragedy!'

'Perhaps I should have taken you to see something more cheerful; but I wanted to see Miss Massey play Lady Macbeth. But let us talk of something else. Splendid fire—is it not?'

Hubert threw off his overcoat, the movement attracted Julia's attention, and it startled her to see how old he seemed to have grown. She noticed as she had not noticed before the grey in his beard and the pathetic weary look that haunted his eyes. And she understood in that instant that the look his face wore was the look of those who have failed in their vocation.

And at that very moment he was wondering if he really loved her, if his marriage were a mistake. The passion he had felt when walking with her on the wet country road he felt no longer, only an undefinable sadness and a weariness which he could not understand. He looked at his wife, and fearing that she divined his thoughts, he kissed her. She returned his kiss coldly and he wondered if she loved him. He thought that it was improbable that she did. Why should she love him? He had never loved any one. He had never inspired love in any one, except perhaps Emily.

'I wonder if you really wished to be married,' she said.

'I always wished to be married,' he replied. 'I hated the Bohemianism I was forced to live in. I longed for a home, for a wife.'

'You were very poor once?'

'Yes: I've lived on tenpence and a shilling a day. I've worked in the docks as a labourer. I went down there hoping to get a clerkship on board one of the Transatlantic steamers. I had had enough of England, and thought of seeking fortune elsewhere.'

'I can hardly believe you worked as a labourer in the docks.'

'Yes; I did. I saw some men going to work, and I joined them. I don't think I thought much about it at the time. A very little misery rubs all the psychology out of us, and we return more easily than one thinks to the animal.'

'And then?'

'At the end of a week the work began to tell upon me, and I drifted back in search of my manuscript.'

'But you must have been in a dreadful condition; your clothes——'

'Ah! thereby hangs a tale. An actress lived in one of the houses I had been lodging in.'

'Oh, tell me about her! This is getting very interesting.'

Then passing his arm round his wife's neck, and with her sweet blonde face looking upon him, and the insinuating warmth of the fire about them, he told her the story of his failure.

'But,' she said, her voice trembling, 'you would not have committed suicide?'

'No man knows beforehand whether he will commit suicide. I can only say that every other issue was closed.'

At the end of a long silence Julia said, 'I wish you hadn't spoken about suicide. I cannot but think of Emily. If she were to make away with herself! The very possibility turns my heart to ice. What should I do—what should we do? I ought never to have given way; we were both abominably selfish. I can see that poor girl sitting alone in that house grieving her heart out.'

'You think that we ought never to have given way!'

'I suppose we ought not. I tried very hard, you know I did. . . . But do you regret?' she said, looking at him suddenly.

'No; I don't regret, but I wish it had happened otherwise.'

'You don't fear anything. Nothing will happen. What can happen?'

'The most terrible things often happen—have happened.'

'Emily may have been fond of me—I think she was; but it was no more than the hysterical caprice of a young girl. Besides, people do not die for love; and I assure you it will be all right. This is not a time for gloomy thoughts.'

'I'll try not to think of her. Well, what were we talking about? I know: about the actress who lived in 17 Fitzroy Street. Tell me about her.'

'She was a real good girl. If she hadn't lent me that five shillings, I don't know where I should be now.'

'Were you very fond of her?'

'No; there never was anything of that sort between us. We were merely friends.'

'And what has become of this actress?'

'You saw her to-night?'

'Was she acting in the piece we saw to-night?'

'It was she who played Lady Macbeth.'

'You are joking.'

'No, I'm not. I always knew she had genius, and they have found it out; but I must say they have taken their time about it.'

'How wonderful! she has succeeded !'

'Yes, *she* has succeeded !'

'And she is really the girl you intended to play Lady Hayward?'

'Yes; and I hope she will play the part one of these days.'

'Of course, she is just the woman for it. What a splendid success she has had! All London is talking about her.'

'And I remember when Ford refused to cast her for the adventuress in *Divorce.* If he had, there is no doubt she would have carried the piece through. Life is but a bundle of chances; she has succeeded, whatever that may mean.'

'But you will let her have the part of Lady Hayward?'

'Yes, of course—that is to say, if——'

'Why "if"?'

'My thoughts are with you, dear; literature seems to have passed out of sight.'

'But you must not sacrifice your talent in worship of me. I shall not allow you. For my sake, if not for hers, you must finish that play. I want you to be famous. I should be for ever miserable if my love proved a upas-tree.'

'A upas-tree! It will be you who will help me; it will be your presence that will help me to write my play. I was always vaguely conscious that you were a necessary element in my life; but I did not wake up to any knowledge of it until that day—do you remember?—when you came into my study to ask me what fish I'd like for dinner, and I begged of you to allow me to read to you that second act. It is that second act that stops me.'

'I thought you had written the second act to your satisfaction. You said that after the talk we had that afternoon you wrote for three hours without stopping, and that you had never done better work.'

'Yes, I wrote a great deal; but on reading it over I found that—I don't mean to say that none of it will stand; some still seems to me to be all right, but a great deal will require alteration.'

The conversation fell. At the end of a long silence Hubert said—

'What are you thinking of, dearest?'

'I was thinking that supposing you were mistaken —if I failed to help you in your work.'

'And I never succeeded in writing my play?'

'No; I don't mean that. Of course you will write your play; all you have to do is to be less critical.'

'Yes, I know—I have heard that before; but, unfortunately, we cannot change ourselves. I'll either carry my play through completely, realise my ideal, or——'

'Remain for ever unsatisfied?'

'Whether I write it or no, I shall be happy in your love.'

'Yes, yes; let us be happy.'

They looked at each other. He did not speak, but his thought said—

'There is no happiness on earth for him who has not accomplished his task.'

'Shall we be happy? I wonder. We have both suffered,' she said, 'we are both tired of suffering, and it is only right that we should be happy.'

'Yes, we shall be happy, I will be happy. It shall be my pleasure to attend to you, to give you all your desire. But you said just now that you had suffered. I have told you my past. Tell me yours. I know nothing except that you were unhappily married.'

'There is little else to know; a woman's life is not adventurous, like a man's. I have not known

the excitement of "first nights," nor the striving and
the craving for an artistic ideal. My life has been
essentially a woman's life,—suppression of self and
monotonous duty, varied by heart-breaking misfortune.
I married when I was very young; before I had even
begun to think about life I found—— But why distress these hours with painful memories?'

'It is pleasant to look back on the troubles we have
passed through.'

'Well, I learnt in one year the meaning of three
terrible words—poverty, neglect, and cruelty. In the
second year of my marriage my husband died of drink,
and I was left a widow at twenty, entirely penniless.
I went to live with my sister, and she was so poor
that I had to support myself by giving music-lessons.
You think you know the meaning of poverty: you
may; but you do not know what a young woman who
wants to earn her bread honestly has to put up with,
trudging through wet and cold, mile after mile, to give
a lesson, paid for at the rate of one-and-sixpence or
two shillings an hour.'

Julia took her eyes from her husband's face, and
looked dreamily into the fire. Then, raising her face
from the flame, she looked around with the air of one
seeking for some topic of conversation. At that

moment she caught sight of the corner of a letter lying on the mantelpiece. Reaching forth her hand, she took it. It was addressed to her husband.

'Here is a letter for you, Hubert. . . . Why, it comes from Ashwood. Yes, and it is in the handwriting of one of the servants. Oh, it is Black's writing! It may be about Emily. Something may have happened to her. Open it quickly.'

'That is not probable. Nothing can have happened to her.'

'Look and see. Be quick!'

Hubert opened the letter, and he had not read three lines when Julia's face caught expression from his, which had become overcast.

'It is bad news, I know. Something has happened. What is it? Don't keep me waiting. The suspense is worse than the truth.'

'It is very awful, Julia. Don't give way.'

'Tell me what it is. Is she dead?

'Yes; she is dead.' Julia got up from her husband's knees and stood by the mantelpiece, leaning upon it. 'It is more than mere death.'

'What do you mean? She killed herself—is that it?'

'Yes; she drowned herself the night before last in the lake.'

'Oh, it is too horrible! Then we have murdered her. Our unpardonable selfishness! I cannot bear it!' Her eyes closed and her lips trembled. Hubert caught her in his arms, laid her on the chair, and, fetching some water in a tumbler, sprinkled her face; then he held it to her lips; she drank a little, and revived. 'I'm not going to faint. Tell me—tell me when the unfortunate child——'

'They don't know exactly. She was in the drawing-room at tea-time, and the drawing-room was empty when Black went round three-quarters of an hour after to lock up. He thought she had gone to her room. It was the gardener who brought in the news in the morning about nine.'

'Oh, good God!'

'Black says he noticed that she looked very depressed the day before, but he thought she was looking better when he brought in the tea.'

'It was then she got my letter. Does Black say anything about giving her a letter?'

'Yes, that is to say——'

'I knew it! I knew it!' said Julia; and her eyes were wild with grief, and she rocked herself to and fro. 'It was that letter that drove her to it. It was most ill-advised. I told you so. You should have written. She would have borne the news better had it come from you. My instinct told me so, but I let myself be persuaded. I told you how it would happen. I told you. You can't say I didn't. Oh! why did you persuade me—why—why—why?'

'Julia dear, we are not responsible. We were in nowise bound to sacrifice our happiness to her——'

'Don't say a word! I say we were bound. Life can never be the same to me again.'

Hubert did not answer. Nothing he could say would be of the slightest avail, and he feared to say anything that might draw from her expressions which she would afterwards regret. He had never seen her moved like this, nor did he believe her capable of such agitation, and the contrast of her present with her usual demeanour made it the more impressive.

'Oh,' she said, leaning forward and looking at him fixedly, 'take this nightmare off my brain, or I shall go mad! It isn't true; it cannot be true. But—oh! yes, it's true enough.'

'Like you, Julia, I am overwhelmed; but we can do nothing.'

'Do nothing!' she cried; 'do nothing! We can do nothing but pray for her—we who sacrificed her.'

And she slipped on her knees and burst into a passionate fit of weeping.

'The best thing that could have happened,' thought Hubert; and his thought said, clearly and precisely, 'Yes; it is awful, shocking, cruel beyond measure!'

The fire was sinking, and he built it up quietly, ashamed of this proof of his regard for physical comfort, and hoping it would pass unnoticed. His pain expressed itself less vehemently than Julia's; but for all that his mind ached. He remembered how he had taken everything from her—fortune, happiness, and now life itself. It was an appalling tragedy—one of those senseless cruelties which we find nature constantly inventing. A thought revealed an unexpected analogy between him and his victim. In both lives there had been a supreme desire, and both had failed. 'Hers was the better part,' he said bitterly. 'Those whose souls are burdened with desire that may not be gratified had better fling the load aside. They are fools who carry it on to the end. . . . If it were not for Julia——'

Then he sought to determine what were his exact feelings. He knew he was infinitely sorry for poor Emily; but he could not stir himself into a paroxysm of grief, and, ashamed of his inability to express his feelings, he looked at Julia, who still wept.

'No doubt,' he thought, 'women have keener feelings than we have.'

. At that moment Julia got up from her knees. She had brushed away her tears. Her face was shaken with grief.

'My heart is breaking,' she said. 'This is too cruel—too cruel! And on my wedding night.'

Their eyes met; and, divining each other's thought, each felt ashamed, and Julia said—

'Oh, what am I saying? This dreadful selfishness, from which we cannot escape, that is with us even in such a moment as this! That poor child gone to her death, and yet amid it all we must think of ourselves.'

'My dear Julia, we cannot escape from our human nature; but, for all that, our grief is sincere. We can do nothing. Do not grieve like that.'

'And why not? She was my best friend. How have I repaid her? Alas! as woman always repays woman for kindness done. The old story. I cannot forgive myself. No, no! do not kiss me! I cannot bear it. Leave me. I can see nothing but Emily's reproachful face.' She covered her face in her hands and sobbed again.'

The same scenes repeated themselves over and over
again. The same fits of passionate grief; the same
moment of calm, when words impregnated with self
dropped from their lips. The same nervous sense
that something of the dead girl stood between them.
And still they sat by the fire, weary with sorrow,
recrimination, long regret, and pain. They could
grieve no more; and before dawn sleep pressed upon
their eyelids, and at the end of a long silence he
dozed—a pale, transparent sleep, through which the
realities of life appeared almost as plainly as before.
Suddenly he awoke, and he shivered in the chill room.
The fire was sinking; dawn divided the window-
curtains. He looked at his wife. She seemed to him
very beautiful as she slept, her face turned a little
on one side, and again he asked himself if he loved
her. Then, going to the window, he drew the curtains
softly, so as not to awaken her; and as he stood
watching a thin discoloured day breaking over the roofs,
it again seemed to him that Emily's suicide was the
better part. 'Those who do not perform their task
in life are never happy.' The words drilled themselves into his brain with relentless insistency. He
felt a terrible emptiness within him which he could
not fill. He looked at his wife and quailed a little

at the thought that had suddenly come upon him. She was something like himself—that was why he had married her. We are attracted by what is like ourselves. Emily's passion might have stirred him. Now he would have to settle down to live with Julia, and their similar natures would grow more and more like one another. Then, turning on his thoughts, he dismissed them. They were the morbid feverish fancies of an exceptional, of a terrible night. He opened the window quietly so as not to awaken his wife. And in the melancholy greyness of the dawn he looked down into the street and wondered what the end would be.

He did not think that he would live long. Disappointed men—those who have failed in their ambition —do not live to make old bones. There were men like him in every profession—the arts are crowded with them. He had met barristers and soldiers and clergymen, just like himself. One hears of their deaths— failure of the heart's action, paralysis of the brain, a hundred other medical causes—but the real cause is, lack of appreciation.

He would hang on for another few years, no doubt; during that time he must try to make his wife happy.

His duty was now to be a good husband, at all events, there was that.

His wife lay asleep in the arm-chair, and fearing she might catch cold, he came into the room closing the window very gently behind him.

THE END

Printed by T. and A. CONSTABLE, Printers to Her Majesty
at the Edinburgh University Press

www.ingramcontent.com/pod-product-compliance
Lightning Source LLC
Chambersburg PA
CBHW030626030726
47497CB00006B/1653